DARK SEAS

DARK SEAS

A WORLD WAR II NOVEL

JERRY BORROWMAN

Covenant Communications, Inc.

Cover image: Edited by Destroyer History Foundation from NARA photo 19-N-57784. Benham (DD 796) stands off new York Navy Yeard, 7 January 1944.

Cover design by Hannah Bischoff. Copyright © 2022 by Covenant Communications, Inc.

Published by Covenant Communications, Inc.
American Fork, Utah

Printed in the United States of America
First Printing: April 2022

28 27 26 25 24 23 22   10 9 8 7 6 5 4 3 2 1

ISBN: 978-1-52441-983-7

PRAISE FOR JERRY BORROWMAN

"*Dark Seas* gives readers tantalizing glimpses of war at sea, and murky dealings by an electronics firm that traded equipment reliability in favor of profits, which in turn endangered lives. Jerry Borrowman has a detailed understanding of Navy ship procedures, and takes readers into the action with a firm hand, making them feel they are actually there. Jerry Borrowman's simple, clear writing will compel readers to turn pages and nod when they reach a satisfying end. Suitable for young readers upwards and those interested in WWII naval stories, *Dark Seas* will not disappoint."

—Readers' Favorite

"Jerry Borrowman has a keen sense of honor and ethics on the battlefield, which serves to provide crucial context—we come to realize a better, rarer definition of hero."

—Foreword Reviews

"Jerry Borrowman brings readers a touch of nostalgia for a time long past, when cars were grand, movies were only shown at theaters, and life moved at a slower pace."

—Jennie Hansen, author *Don't Say a Word*

CHAPTER ONE

A POINT SOUTH OF ICELAND;
MERCHANT MARINE

April 1942

"You there! What are you doing here? You have no business in this part of the ship."

Ordinary seaman Joseph Horiuchi bristled. As a Japanese American who was born and raised in Boston, he was used to this type of treatment. It was par for the course. Still, even as one of the few Japanese men serving in the Merchant Marine, he had been treated fairly well by nearly everyone here on the freighter *MaryAnn*, with the exception of his current antagonist, Communications Specialist Able Seaman Brad Winters, who was now challenging him. Everything about Winters was indicative of a bully.

"Seaman Horiuchi doing assigned maintenance work," Joe reported. "Someone with seasickness vomited in the passageway, and I was ordered here to clean it up." He did not need to add the last sentence since it was enough to say he was there by assignment. But he suspected that it was Winters who had lost his lunch in the unusually heavy seas, and Joe wanted to let Winters know his fragile stomach had forced Joe to come clean up the mess.

Courtesy would have dictated a reply, but Winters just shrugged and turned back to the book he was reading while seated in front of the radio equipment. The part that rankled Joe the most was that he knew Winters to be incompetent at his job. Joe felt fully qualified to make that judgment; before the war, he was one of the first students enrolled in the Rensselaer Polytechnic Institute in Troy, New York, in the new specialty of electronics.

Had the war not broken out, he would have pursued a degree with the help of neighbors and friends back in Boston, who were anxious to help him be one of the first Japanese *Nisei*—a second-generation Japanese person born in America to Japanese immigrant parents—to graduate from such a prestigious American school. Though highly unusual, it was not impossible for a Nisei to be accepted at a handful of schools, like Rensselaer, but he'd had to prove exceptional ability for it to happen.

Then came the war and the anti-Japanese hysteria on the West Coast that led to internment camps. Joe was in danger wherever he went. Acting quickly, he chose to enlist in the Merchant Marine instead of waiting to be drafted into an all-Nisei unit in the United States Army. Joe had heard there was less discrimination in the Merchant Marine than in the regular military services. No matter how successful one of the Japanese units were in the army, people viewed them with suspicion and made false accusations of the Nisei being traitors to America. Not a single case had ever been found of any Japanese American, first or second generation, ever spying for Japan. But prejudice caused by their physical appearance caused them to be treated differently than even German Americans, among whom espionage *had* been found. Joe's decision to choose the Merchant Marine had been a good experience, by and large, with the exception of working with a handful of boors like Brad Winters.

As an ordinary seaman, it was the task of Joe and others of his rank to do all the hard, physical work of the ship. That included custodial duties as well as repair and maintenance, such as scraping and painting in the never-ending battle against rust.

If the cargo moved in a storm, Joe's group manhandled it back into place. If a piece of the ship's equipment was damaged, Joe and his crew had to fix or isolate it. Kitchen duties, cleaning the toilets in the head, throwing the trash overboard—it all fell to men like Joe. Perhaps that was why the injury rate was highest among the ordinary seamen. The "able" seaman, on the other hand, had specialized jobs, like communications, and they were only occasionally forced to do hard physical labor and, even then, mostly in emergencies. Winters had proved himself adept at getting out of even that kind of work—he either feigned an injury or tried to act like he was the officer in charge of managing the situation. Joe did not feel anger so much as disgust at Winters.

Of course, he could never say anything to anyone about it. It was not a Japanese man's place to criticize a white man, no matter how justified the criticism. Though he was recognized as a good and steady worker, few of the crew wanted to be seen talking with Joe since doing so would jeopardize their social standing. Joe spent most of his time alone with his thoughts, eating at a table by himself and talking to others only when it was called for. The fact that he was smart, well read, and clever meant nothing onboard the *MaryAnn*. He was on the lowest rung of the social ladder—maybe not even *on* the ladder yet— and that's just how it was.

Later that night, after cleaning up Winters's vomit and completing his kitchen duties, Joe retired to his spot in the crew cabin, where others were playing cards, and started doing what he loved most—working on the broken-down radio sets he had purchased in Halifax, Nova Scotia, at the beginning of the voyage. It was hard to do in rough seas, but it was now sunset, and the ocean was settling in that unusual calm that prevailed nearly every day at both sunrise and sunset. So, he was working as fast as possible to solder a new set of wires to the least-damaged radio chassis before the waves picked up again. He hoped that he could increase its reception range through a design he had thought up earlier that day.

"May I ask what you're working on?"

Joe instinctively jumped at the sound, which brought an apology. Turning, Joe was startled to see the captain. Joe stood up awkwardly to face him. "Just working on a hobby of mine, sir. I enjoy working on radios and other electronic equipment." Joe was shaken to have the captain of the ship speak to him directly—it was so out of the ordinary as to border on the impossible; captains always spoke through their subordinate officers. Plus, it drew unwanted attention his way. Still, one could not refuse to speak to the captain. He shifted his weight, waiting for the captain's response.

"An interesting hobby. What exactly are you doing? It looks like you're working on two different radios."

"Yes, sir—three actually. They are all nonfunctioning, which is how I could afford to buy them in Halifax. My hope is to take parts from each of the damaged sets to build one working radio. I'm also trying to design it in such a way that it is more powerful than any of the original sets." He sighed. "I'm not sure I can do it, but it's an interesting puzzle to try to figure out."

Captain Jim Birdsall furrowed his brow. Seeing such initiative was unusual. Most of his ordinary seaman were in another corner of the deck playing cards. Birdsall thought it even more unusual that Seaman Horiuchi was the one taking initiative. One of the things Birdsall liked most about the Merchant Marine is that, with a crew of just fifty men, he could learn the names of everyone serving onboard. That was impossible for the captain of a US Navy ship, where the crew numbered in the hundreds or even thousands.

"May I ask where you learned how to do this? It seems quite technical."

Joe decided to throw caution to the wind. He could not fall any lower in the pecking order, after all. "You can ask me any question you'd like, sir. I learned about radios in high school back in Boston. My parents were both professors at Tufts University, and I spent a year at Rensselaer Polytechnic in New York before joining the service. I planned to get a degree in electronics." He suspected this would shock the captain, but who cared? It was the truth.

"You don't say." Birdsall smiled. "I graduated from Rensselaer myself in mechanical engineering because electronics were just coming on the scene. But it was a top-rate education, to be sure. I'm sorry you had to leave."

Joe shook his head to clear his now-jumbled thoughts as he realized that he had to confront his own prejudice. "Really, I didn't know."

Birdsall smiled again. "I know what you're thinking: why would a Rensselaer-trained engineer settle for the Merchant Marine?" He held up his hand to stop Joe from protesting. "I get that a lot, so don't worry." He motioned to a chair next to the small worktable where Joe had his equipment laid out and asked if he could sit down with his cup of tea.

This caused Joe's head to spin even more since no white person had ever treated him with such courtesy. Joe nodded in the affirmative and then sat down in his own chair after waiting for Captain Birdsall to sit in his. The captain brought his tea to his lips, then set his cup down.

"Here's the story," the captain continued. "I was one of the first to enroll in the Naval Reserve Officers Training Corp. My parents were working-class people and could not afford to send me to the kind of school I wanted to attend, so I viewed the NROTC as the best way to get help paying for tuition. Growing up in Nebraska, I was always fascinated by stories of the sea, so I thought I'd enjoy the navy more than the army."

He shrugged. "I'm not sure it was the best choice, but it was the choice I made. After graduation, I went on active duty and enjoyed being a naval officer. Then I was in an accident; my left leg was crushed when a depth charge launcher malfunctioned, and—just that fast—I was out of the navy with a disability. I now walk with a limp. But I like living and working at sea, so I signed on with the Merchant Marine—they choose not to notice the limp. The pay is good, particularly now, in wartime. And that's how I came to be here with you in the Merchant Marine, the branch of service that can proudly claim the highest casualty rate of the war."

He smiled. "But I still like it, despite the risks. I cannot imagine that anyone is doing more to help win the war than we are. Right now, Britain is the only thing standing between Hitler and his complete domination of Europe. And the only way Britain can survive is if we keep doing our job of bringing supplies, food, and equipment to England." The captain sat back in his chair and then smiled. "I'm sure that's far more than you wanted to know, but it's enjoyable for me to speak with someone who appreciates engineering as much as I do. Though our paths have been different, we have our education in common and now this."

"That is an impressive story." Joe shook his head slightly. He was embarrassed that he had misjudged this man—and perhaps others on the ship. He had viewed the Merchant Marine as the low end of service with the slow, steaming cargo ships plodding their way across the ocean with virtually no way to defend themselves. But looking at it the way Birdsall described it, perhaps it was the most daring place to be—certainly the riskiest. "Thank you for sharing that with me, sir. It gives me even greater confidence in what we are doing."

Birdsall stood, and Joe followed suit. "Well," Birdsall said, "I've taken you away from your task too long. It's nice to talk with a fellow alumnus."

Joe assumed that was his coded way of saying a *well-educated man.*

"I gather that those are shortwave radios?"

"Yes, sir."

"You don't plan on doing any broadcasting . . ."

"No, sir. Listen only. I understand the need for radio silence on our part."

"Very good. Would you mind keeping me posted on your progress? If it turns out that you do build a more powerful set, I might ask to use it on occasion to listen in on what is happening back home—only occasionally, I promise. I just can't tie up the ship's radio for that."

Joe smiled. He could not help himself. "I'd be happy to do that, sir. Who knows? Maybe I can build two sets from three— one for each of us."

Birdsall nodded and then withdrew.

"Well, that was unexpected," Joe said quietly to himself. As he turned back to the workbench, he noticed that the men playing cards were looking his way. Was that good or bad news? Either they would see him in a positive new light, or they would be angry that he'd been talking to someone above his station. "I'll find out soon enough." Experience told him it probably would not turn out well.

* * *

Joe was fast asleep when the explosion came. One moment he was dreaming, and the next he was screaming. He struggled to gain his bearings in the dark while he jumped at the sound of the Klaxon horn blasting out the all-hands-on-deck signal. Even though it was urgent, he took a few moments to feel his entire body to see if he was injured. By now, he was able to guess that the blast had been toward the stern, and after confirming that he was uninjured, he swung his legs over the side of the hammock and pulled his trousers on quickly. He wished the lighting would come on so he could see where he was going, but there was no sign that was going to happen. So, he made his way in the dark, suddenly grateful for all the time he had spent swabbing the corridors as he realized that he had a complete mental map of the ship.

He was surprised that he did not encounter more men along the way. But at 10,000 tons, the *MaryAnn* was a large ship for a crew of only fifty. Most of the crew worked in the engine room, where, by Joe's guess, most of them had likely been killed by the torpedo.

There should be a passageway up to the deck about right here. Sure enough, his hands detected a corner, and he turned and shuffled his feet until they hit the rung of the ladder. Making his way up to the next deck, he started to see some light farther along the corridor—the radio shack had its own emergency power supply. As he made his way toward the front of the corridor, he heard an argument. Then Joe watched in shock as Winters shoved Captain Birdsall out of the radio room and back against the wall of the corridor. Winters then turned toward the exit out to the deck and shoved Joe as he raced past. Surer of himself now, Joe started running toward the spot where the captain had been assaulted.

"Are you all right, sir?"

Birdsall turned at the sound of his voice, clearly rattled by the encounter. "Mr. Horiuchi, what are you doing here?"

"Following orders, sir. All-hands-on-deck. This is the shortest route from my bunk."

"Ah, yes." The captain was flustered. Who wouldn't be with the ship hit by at least one torpedo and with no way to know if another was on the way?

"Did Mr. Winters attack you, sir?" Joe knew the answer but thought this was a better way to get the captain talking.

Birdsall turned and studied him. "Mr. Horiuchi, that doesn't matter now. Do you know how to send out a distress signal?"

Joe's eyes widened. "Yes, sir. I'm sure I can figure it out."

Birdsall placed his hands firmly on Joe's shoulders and pushed him into the radio room. "Excellent. I want you to send out a message with an SOS and our coordinates. We need to warn the convoy that a U-boat has struck so they can take evasive action. And maybe one of the ships can stop just long enough to rescue us." Birdsall began writing on a piece of paper.

"Of course." Joe moved immediately to the radio gear. Although he had never worked on this specific type of set before, he made a quick assessment and then looked down at the code book to find the appropriate frequency. Once he figured that out, he turned some dials and then looked up at Captain Birdsall. "I'm ready to send whenever you give the command."

"Send this." Birdsall held out the written message. "Keep sending until you receive an acknowledgement, which will probably be a single word." He waited until this registered with Joe. "The escort ships won't want to give away their position, so they'll send a single word—not enough for the U-boats to triangulate their position. But it will let you know that your message has been received."

"Yes, sir." Joe turned to start the transmission.

"And, Mr. Horiuchi, do you have a watch?"

Joe reached inside his vest pocket and pulled out a pocket watch.

"Good. Mark the time and start sending. But under no circumstance are you to stay here more than ten minutes. We are taking on water and will sink. I want you up to the lifeboats in twelve minutes. Do you understand?"

"Yes, sir. Twelve minutes to the lifeboat."

Birdsall stared at him. "Mr. Horiuchi, do not disobey this order out of a sense of misguided heroism. If you are not there, I will come back for you, and that could cost both of us our lives." Birdsall suspected that Joe was the type to sacrifice himself despite orders, and he did not want that for this man.

For his part, Joe understood Birdsall's suspicion and was . . . he struggled to find the word . . . *grateful* that the captain would insist that he save himself. And if he didn't, the captain would risk his own life to save a Japanese ordinary seaman. Such a thing was unheard of. So, rather than betray the emotion he felt, Joe replied crisply, "Ten minutes of transmission, two minutes to the boats. I'll be there!"

"Very well." With that, Birdsall turned and started running, most likely to the bridge to sound the abandon-ship signal and destroy all his ships logs. No sense giving the Germans any accidental intelligence from recovered documents.

Now Joe turned to the radio set and started broadcasting on the long-wave ship-to-ship radio. He repeated Birdsall's words exactly, including their position. After sending these four times in succession, he listened intently but received no reply.

"Gotta try something else," Joe muttered. Spying an old Morse code key, he decided to take a chance on that. Morse code had a wider broadcasting range, and it was likely the convoy had moved away from them since the *MaryAnn* had been hit. He repeated the same message in Morse code, the dots and dashes coming quite naturally to him. After doing this twice, he was startled to hear his own key start bouncing in reply. "Received," was all the message said. "That's good enough!"

Joe was exultant. He had made their condition and position known.

Now a new shock hit him when he glanced down at his pocket watch and saw that nine minutes had elapsed. He had been so intent on sending his messages that he had lost sense of time. He stood up and moved into the corridor, where he turned left and started jogging toward the hatch that would lead him out and onto the deck. But just as he was about to open the door, the world tore itself apart. In the most incredibly painful moment of his life, Joe felt a blast that sent him flying into the bulkhead wall behind him, and he felt something stab him in the back as he fell. Worse still was the incredible, deafening pressure on his ears. He was finally able to shake his head to try to figure out where he was and discovered that he was lying on his back with a metal something pinning him to the floor.

Even though he still could not hear his own voice, he talked to himself out loud as a way to steady his nerves. "You've got to get out of here, Joseph! That was a second torpedo!" 'Joseph'— that is how his mother always addressed him when something serious was happening. He pushed against the metal to clear himself but was only able to make it move a few inches. *Okay, this is a problem!* He was able to move his legs, so he struggled to bring them into a position where he could push against the obstruction. This started to have an effect, but it was not fast enough. With a new hole in its side, the *MaryAnn* was already listing badly to port, and Joe knew that if he did not get out of there fast, the ship could turn turtle—upside down—and trap him. "You have to make this happen," he said through clenched teeth, but no matter how hard he struggled, he could not work himself clear.

His fear turned to panic as he realized that he was not likely to escape. The thought of being trapped as the ship went under the water was terrifying. "Oh, dear God, please help me!" Joe was not a particularly religious man, although his parents had always taken him to church. But right now, he was desperate.

That is when he heard a very faint voice call out, "Joe, are you there? Joe Horiuchi, are you there?"

He started breathing so fast that it was hard to get any words out. "I'm here! I'm here! There's something across my legs that I can't get out from under!" He wished his hearing was not so impaired—there was a terrible ringing sound that made it difficult to sort out the words. As it turned out, he did not need his hearing, for in just a moment, he saw some flashlights in the corridor and then several dark figures working to free him. Pushing with all the strength he had, he felt the object start to move, and then suddenly, as if by magic, he was free. "It worked!" he shouted. "I'm out."

Strong hands from those in the captain's party reached down and pulled him into a standing position.

"We've got to get out right now!" Joe heard this clearly because Captain Birdsall shouted it directly into his left ear. Joe allowed Birdsall to guide him as they made their way forward and then turned out to the deck. At this point, he knew that the regular lifeboat was useless; the ship was overturning in such a way that they were on the high side of the listing, making it impossible to lower a lifeboat. He hoped some of the men had gotten off on the port side before the list was too great.

"Come with me," Birdsall said firmly as he led the small group of survivors toward the port side. "Everybody needs to grab something that floats and then get ready to slide into the water. I've got a flare that I'll shoot up, and then you go." He turned to Joe, probably sensing that he was having trouble with his hearing. "Did you get that, Mr. Horiuchi?"

Joe nodded and said that he understood. Then he moved away from Birdsall to find something that would float. It was a hard task on a ship made of metal, but at the last moment, he spied a rope chest made of wood. Stumbling toward it in the semi-darkness—dawn was now approaching—he managed to clear the ropes from inside and then positioned himself for the slide into the water. There were many potential obstacles between his position on the deck and the water, so he plotted the path he would try to follow to control the slide.

Then he heard a subdued popping sound, followed by Birdsall's shouting, "Go! Everybody go!"

As he started sliding, he realized that Birdsall had made them all wait so they would be close to each other in the water and easier to rescue—if a rescue was in the cards. With a U-boat still lurking under the waves, it was doubtful any of the other ships in the convoy would risk it. "But that will have to wait!" he said out loud. It was something of a novelty to hear his own voice so muffled.

Joe was fortunate in that he was able to maneuver around the obstacles because of his planning. He watched as one of the other men smashed into a ventilation vent as the angle of the deck had steepened sharply. Joe would have helped him, but it was impossible. He had already slid past the man's position.

As Joe moved faster and faster, he braced for the moment when he would hit the water, but there was really no way to prepare. He couldn't help but inhale sharply as he and his wooden chest slammed into the freezing-cold water of the North Atlantic. In just a moment, he was gasping for air as he bobbed up from going under the surface. His rope chest had floated away while he was flailing in the water, so he started ferociously swimming after it. The movement of swimming helped him warm up a bit, so he kept up the pace—particularly when he saw another man swimming for his chest! "Oh, no you don't!" But the other fellow was closer, and before Joe could get there, the other man claimed it. In a fury unlike anything he had ever experienced in his life, Joe swam even faster to knock the man off and reclaim his chest. Even as he did so, his mind was telling him that the chest had more than enough wood for both, but his indignation drove him forward.

His thoughts raced. Why would the other fellow reason with Joe? This man had the chest, and it did not matter how he came to possess it! Why would he yield even part of it to Joe Horiuchi, the lowest man on the ship? All of this crossed his mind in the few moments that he was swimming, and it increased his anger with each stroke. He went nearly crazy when he got close enough to see that it was Brad Winters who had stolen his rope chest.

So intent was he on making his way to the expected confrontation that for a moment he failed to notice the giant shadow that fell across Winters. But when he did see the shadow, he looked up and shouted. "Get out of the way, Winters! Get out of the way!"

Rather than look up to see the danger, Winters just sneered at him and made an obscene gesture.

Joe tried again. "Move out of the way!"

But it was too late. Joe heard the crash, even with his deafened ears, and then felt a massive turbulence in the water as the ship's gigantic funnel toppled into the water, smashing into Winters and the sea chest, driving them under the water and out of sight. The smokestack missed Joe by just a few yards. The wash of the wave came crashing into him, sending him reeling backward. Once he righted himself in the water, he looked in horror as the funnel settled in the water, enough air trapped inside to freeze it in that position. But the man—Brad Winters—did not come back up. Joe's mind raced as he realized that he had just witnessed the death of the man he despised most, his death a result of clinging to the chest that Joe had been intent on taking from him. Had Joe succeeded in reaching the chest . . .

Joe started crying. Not out of remorse and not even out of guilt. It was all just too much. Awakened by an explosion, trapped in a corridor, freezing in the water, and consumed by jealousy and the desire for revenge—it was just overwhelming. So, he cried—something he hadn't allowed himself to do since he was a child.

And he treaded the water. After a moment's reflection, he was convinced that Winters was the lucky one. Winters was now dead, but it could take an hour or more before Joe froze to death. But then, this thought prompted one of his internal debates with himself: *It won't take hours. Use your head, Joe! You'll freeze to death in a few minutes. You know that!* He struggled to conjure up the formula for how long a man could survive in the waters of the North Atlantic before hypothermia robbed him of consciousness. It was a useful diversion of his thought, but thinking about it was hard, so he closed his eyes. He resolved he would hold out to the very end. He felt himself start to shiver and was somehow grateful that his body was trying to stay alive. Then he wondered what death would bring. Some people said a beautiful light welcomed you into heaven. He suspected everything would just go dark, ending in a complete loss of consciousness. Either way, he was sorry that it had come to this.

And then, at the height of feeling sorry for himself, he felt something jar up against him. With no idea what it could be, he jerked his eyes open just in time to see a pair of hands reaching over the side of a lifeboat to pull him in.

This really was too much to process. How was this even possible? But he was a willing accomplice and did his best to help his benefactor. As he came sliding over the side and into the bottom of the boat with a great splash of water, he looked up to see Captain Birdsall smiling at him. "That was a close one, Mr. Horiuchi! The old *MaryAnn* almost smashed you into eternity."

"Yes, sir. But how . . ."

Birdsall swept his hand to indicate the others in the boat. "These good men rescued me, and I asked them to rescue you. They were smart enough to get off on the right side of the ship." He paused for just a moment. "Now tell me, did you get the signal off? Was it acknowledged?"

"Morse—Morse code." Joe's teeth were chattering from the cold. "I didn't get a response to the long-wave radio broadcast, probably because the ships were out of range, but I decided to send the message by code, and I got a single word response: Received. That's when I started for the deck."

Birdsall nodded. The sky was now light enough that nearly everything was visible. "That's good. I'm not sure they can rescue us, but at least we have a chance." He turned to the other men in the boat. "Mr. Horiuchi here sent out our distress signal after that scoundrel Winters abandoned his post as a coward. If we are rescued, it is because of Joe Horiuchi, here." If Birdsall thought this would bring a cheer from the others in the boat, he was disappointed, for the men just nodded sullenly. Joe imagined that at least some of them had grumbled when Birdsall ordered them to rescue him. But now they at least knew Joe had done his part.

"All right. Let's start bailing this thing out so we can stay as dry as possible. I've sent up a flare, and Mr. Horiuchi sent our distress signal, so we should see someone soon."

Joe couldn't tell if Birdsall really believed that, but it was the right thing to say in the circumstance. Joe moved to an open spot on the side so that he could help row if the need arose. But for the moment, he pulled his arms and legs close together to conserve as much warmth as possible. He was in the North Atlantic in the middle of winter. But at least he was not alone.

CHAPTER TWO
THE ATLANTIC

May 1942

IS THIS AN ATTACK OR mutual suicide? Given the high-stakes nature of this convoy patrol, with dozens of ships carrying foodstuffs, munitions, and fuel to America's beleaguered allies in Great Britain, it mattered a great deal whether Captain Merrill Kendrick's destroyer could find and destroy the U-boats that had earlier attacked one of the merchant ships in the convoy. But the nature of "destroyer versus U-boat" was complicated, with the two ships trying desperately to escape each other, while simultaneously looking for an opportunity to turn and attack.

Which is why he had asked himself this mental question—attack or suicide? It was a question Kendrick often wondered, given the ability of a U-boat being pursued by an Allied destroyer to turn into an attack position during a long battle. Pursuer and pursued changed roles frequently in this life-and-death game. Kendrick used his right hand to rub the back of his neck while looking down at his left wrist to see what time it was. "Three and a half hours and we still haven't got them."

"No, sir. But I'm positive our last attack wounded them."

Kendrick licked the salt spray off his lips. He hated that because it would make him thirsty, but what else was there to do? "I hope so," he replied to First Officer Lieutenant Henry Farrell. "If we did damage him, he should be struggling with his underwater speed."

"Yes, sir," said Farrell as he peered through his binoculars. It was just before sunup, and everyone's eyes were adjusting to the increased light as they sailed directly toward the coming sunrise. That would present a new set of challenges in their surface observations.

Kendrick furrowed his brow, trying to create a mental map of all the maneuvers they had made to this point in time to better estimate where the German U-boat would be just now. But a conversation he had once had with his father intruded on his thoughts. After Merrill had told his father about a similar sub chase on an earlier voyage, Vernon Kendrick had replied that it was just like stalking wild game at their summer home in Maine. But Merrill knew the analogy was flawed. Never once had a deer turned to attack the hunter, while a U-boat was constantly maneuvering to get a shot off with its torpedoes, either at the destroyer chasing it or one of the ships in the convoy the destroyer was trying to shield. It was a dangerous game in which the hunter could quickly become the prey by making just one false turn while overrunning the enemy's position.

"Come right five degrees rudder."

"Come right five degrees rudder—aye, aye, sir!" the helmsman responded. This allowed Kendrick to correct the order if it was misunderstood.

A few moments later, the helmsman barked, "Completed turn to ninety-five degrees." This meant they were now heading just slightly south of due east.

"Very well." Kendrick said this without any conscious thought. It was part of the procedure to make sure everyone on the bridge understood orders issued and completed. It also allowed Kendrick, as the conning officer, to keep his mental map of the situation in good order. *Conning* was the naval term for setting course and speed. Navigation at sea was given in two formats: if the command was stated in increments of 360 degrees, it meant they were using the compass to indicate which direction a ship should go—north, south, east, or west; if it was given as a "come to," it meant to deviate by that many points from their current course. All officers and enlisted men on the bridge knew these protocols so well that they did not even consciously think about it.

We dropped depth charges ten minutes ago, Kendrick thought. *Then we started a wide sweep to starboard, which I just tightened. If they were damaged, they would turn . . .* It was impossible to know which way they had turned. But based on the U-boat's actions throughout the battle, it was likely they would have turned to port to bring them closer to the convoy—assuming the U-boat was undamaged. That move would increase the U-boat's danger, but this German *Kapitänleutnant* (captain lieutenant) had always chosen the most aggressive path.

That was why Kendrick had finally succeeded in crossing above him and dropping a spread of depth charges on the overconfident U-boat; from Kendrick's point of view, unpredictability was of far greater value in a cat-and-mouse game than boldness. *But if he was damaged, he will likely turn to starboard to put some distance between them and the dangers lurking above.* Kendrick had made his broad turn to starboard, meaning he shared Lieutenant Farrell's suspicion that the U-boat was wounded. *If only there were a way to know!*

This had been an unusual battle in that Kendrick had been forced to leave the other three destroyers under his command scattered far afield to protect the large ships of the convoy. Two were tankers carrying fuel oil that the British navy desperately needed, so their protection was paramount. That meant Kendrick had chased the U-boat on his own, which was an extremely dubious exercise for his old, outdated destroyer. The *USS Lester* was a World War I four-stack relic.

Bringing his mind back to the battle, he accepted that not only did he have to locate the exact position of the U-boat to initiate the attack, he also had to guess its depth in order to bring the depth charges close enough to the sub to damage it.

If he was off—even by just twenty yards—$30,000 of depth charges would explode harmlessly out of range of the U-boat. Unlike horseshoes, close was not good enough in anti-submarine warfare. You had to have a ringer—or at least a leaner—to cause any damage. To make matters worse, this was the third chase of this voyage, which meant he was running low on depth charges.

Kendrick sighed. It was a big ocean with lots of room to maneuver, so it seemed that the U-boat commander held the upper hand.

"Right handsomely," Kendrick said, indicating they needed to make a slight adjustment in the steering to bring it to the previously ordered position.

"Right handsomely—aye, aye sir," responded the helm.

By now they had made their way through half of the large, sweeping circle that had taken them away from the convoy. In Kendrick's mind, he could imagine the U-boat turning away from the last point of contact. If Kendrick had guessed right, they should cross the U-boat in another five minutes.

"Sonar reports contact bearing dead ahead, range unknown," the telephone talker said.

"Very well."

"So, you guessed correctly," Farrell said.

Kendrick displayed the slightest hint of a smile. "Maybe. We should know for sure in about sixty seconds."

"Sonar confirms contact, bearing five degrees off port, range 3,000," said the talker in his intentionally monotonous voice.

"Very well. Left seven degrees rudder." Kendrick said this evenly, not wanting his voice to betray his excitement. Kendrick turned to his chief gunnery officer. "Set charges for shallow, a three-charge spread."

"Set to shallow, three-charge spread—aye, aye, sir!"

He wished he could fire just one depth charge with absolute certainty it would hit, but the stakes were too high—he would have to hazard three to increase his chance of a hit.

Kendrick turned to First Officer Farrell. "I'm going with your assessment that he was damaged, Henry. He's not likely to have gone deep if he's got any leaks."

"Yes, sir."

Kendrick could tell his words simultaneously pleased Farrell, as he was being taken seriously, and increased his anxiety in case he was wrong.

"Contact bearing two degrees off starboard, range 1,500 yards."

"Very well." The *Lester* was now leading the U-boat, but it was too soon to know the speed of the German vessel. A further course correction was likely.

It was at this point that Kendrick's mind registered the fact that he had not heard the helm confirm his earlier turn to port. "How is your rudder?" he demanded of the helm.

The voice of the helmsman was flustered as he replied, "Steady on course, eighty-eight degrees!" That meant the earlier command had been executed but not confirmed. Kendrick was quite certain no further reproof would be required for this lapse, given the anxiety in the young man's voice.

"Radar reports contact dead ahead, range 1,000."

"Very well." Kendrick ordered a further slight turn to port as he was not gaining on the U-boat fast enough. "Increase speed to full ahead!"

"Increase speed to full ahead—aye, aye, sir," confirmed the lee helmsman.

Kendrick heard the command repeated verbally and glanced to the side as the brass repeater was thrust forward to the neutral position, then backed to "full ahead." This same sequence would be repeated on a similar device in the engine room. Though he did not really need verbal confirmation that the command was received since he felt a change in the tempo of the vibration underfoot, the lee helmsman had followed proper protocol. "Very well."

"Lieutenant Farrell, please have the lookouts keep an extra sharp eye for periscopes. So far, we've only been fighting this one fellow, but enough time has elapsed for others to come up."

"Aye, aye, sir." Farrell moved off the bridge to the wings to personally deliver the command and to give his own pass with the binoculars. The *Lester* was most vulnerable while on the attack since it had to maintain a constant speed and bearing— the perfect opportunity for another U-boat to launch torpedoes.

"Prepare to fire, Mr. Pendleton!" Chief Gunnery Officer Don Pendleton was the *Lester's* no-nonsense man, whom Kendrick judged to be very proficient at his job.

"Aye, aye, sir. Ready at your command!"

"Radar reports contact dead ahead, range unknown."

"Very well." This meant that they were so close to the target that radar could no longer give an accurate reading.

"Fire!"

He heard Pendleton repeat the order, and Kendrick started counting to measure the time until the depth charges would explode.

"Torpedoes approaching off the port bow!" Farrell shouted.

Kendrick whirled to see for himself and quickly realized that a second U-boat had, indeed, fired forward of them, expecting to strike at midships.

"Hard right rudder!"

"Hard right rudder—aye, aye, sir!"

"Full reverse starboard engine!"

The order was confirmed. This maneuver would make the tightest possible turn to starboard; the port propeller on the left side would be moving forward while the starboard propeller on the right side would be pulling that side of the ship backward. Just like driving a tractor and turning sharply by stopping the large wheel on the side the driver wishes to turn. Kendrick hoped it would pull their bow at the front of the ship out of the path of the German torpedoes.

"Hard right rudder, confirmed!" This time the helm's report was superfluous, but the lesson had been learned.

"Tell the men to brace for impact!"

This command was repeated through the loudspeaker system, although most of the men did not need the warning. At the instant both turning commands were executed, the ship started into a sharp thirty-five-degree turn to starboard, which was the maximum a destroyer could take without swamping. Men all over the ship were now grabbing for something to steady themselves as the ship leaned sharply into the turn.

As the ship met the turn, Kendrick registered the explosion of the three depth charges, now off of the starboard side. He also saw the track of the torpedoes and ordered, "All engines ahead, flank speed," which was confirmed and executed. But he knew in a moment that it would not be enough. Even at top speed, he had no chance of outrunning the torpedoes, and at least two would hit them with a glancing blow.

Kendrick turned to his radio operator. "Message to the *Williams*: 'Am attacking one U-boat but am under attack by a second. Likely to be hit by torpedoes. Break off and move against the second German. Estimated position is . . .'" He paused as the navigator provided the coordinates to the radioman, and thus to the captain of the *USS Williams*, the Allied destroyer closest to the *Lester*.

"Understood," replied the captain of the *Williams*. "Am turning to intercept new target. Good luck, *Lester*!"

"Thank you!" Kendrick's reply was brief. He then turned his attention back to the battle at hand.

"Let's hope they're duds like so many of the German torpedoes," Farrell said.

Kendrick registered this wish from Farrell, but he suspected it was not to be.

"Would you look at that?"

Kendrick turned at the sound of the young ensign's voice. He was looking off the stern. There, indeed, was a sight not often seen. In the spot where the depth charges had landed, the water was bubbling and frothing as the bow of the German U-boat arced up and out of the water, falling with a great splash as gravity asserted itself.

"You got him, sir!" Farrell shouted. "We got him!"

Kendrick surveyed the scene to see if the U-boat could bring deck guns to bear but relaxed as he saw German sailors come streaming out on the deck. They wanted out of there as quickly as possible. It was a welcome sight.

Returning his thoughts to the torpedoes racing toward the *Lester*, he repeated Farrell's phrase in his mind. *Those torpedoes could be duds!* He hoped they were. "Stand steady!" Their emergency turn had protected the heart of the ship, but a strike on the stern was now inevitable. Had the twenty-five-year-old *Lester* been capable of just a little more speed, they might have escaped. Kendrick winced as an explosion rocked the rear of the ship.

"Radio message to the *Williams*: 'We have been hit. Will report damage when known. Do not, repeat, do not move to assist until you've dealt with the other U-boat.'"

"*Lester*, aye, aye, sir. We have plotted the trail of the torpedoes and are moving to intercept. Will do our best to neutralize the threat."

"Very well." He slashed across his throat to indicate to the radioman to break the connection with the *Williams*. The last thing its captain needed was to be distracted by unnecessary chatter from Kendrick.

"Damage report!"

"Damage to the rudder and to the port screw, sir! The chief engineer has ordered all stop to prevent further damage."

"Very well." Kendrick turned to Farrell. "I need you to go down there and see if we're seaworthy. Get the men out and seal the watertight doors if needed."

"Aye, aye, sir." Farrell was off in an instant.

"Mr. Pendleton, we're a sitting duck for that U-boat's torpedoes right now, but there's not much we can do about it.

Do order your gunners to stand ready on the off chance that the *Williams* is able to force her to the surface."

"Aye, aye, sir. Guns to the ready."

Next, he turned to the ensign. "Mr. Carroll, get down on deck and prepare to take any German prisoners on board that make their way to us. Follow standard protocol to protect the ship's crew."

"Aye, aye, sir. Prepare to accept German prisoners." There was a puzzled tone to the young man's voice, but he moved quickly to complete the order.

"Our best chance of avoiding another torpedo is to be seen taking on the Germans," Kendrick said in response to the surprised looks of the helmsman and lee helmsman. He felt slightly vindicated when understanding lifted their expressions. The helmsman was responsible for steering the ship; the lee helmsman managed communications with the engine room to control speed and direction of the propellers, forward or reverse.

Of course, an aggressive German U-boat captain would torpedo us anyway—the chance of killing an American warship is worth far more than saving a German crew that will be taken into captivity. Still, there was nothing he could do about it, so he moved out to the wing to follow the action of the *Williams* as it bore down on the other U-boat.

"Are there still more U-boats now moving in to attack the convoy?" he asked himself, now out of reach of listening ears.

A messenger stepped onto Kendrick's outside deck, "Captain, the chief engineer pays his respects and says he can give you all ahead slow on the right propeller."

"Very well." Kendrick acknowledged the messenger, not fully able to conceal his excitement at this new development. Having the use of even one propeller meant they were no longer dead in the water, and he could execute some protective maneuvers if attacked. He immediately stepped back onto the bridge. "Ahead slow, hard left rudder—or as much as you can get out of the rudder."

At this point, Kendrick was ever so glad he had sent Farrell down below. With the right screw turning and with any help they could get from the rudder, the *Lester* would swing to port and narrow its profile to the other U-boat. It was a slender hope, but facing them directly would make it more difficult for the U-boat to hit them with a second spread of torpedoes. Plus, it would expose all the Germans swimming in the ocean to any torpedo that went past the *Lester*, which just might discourage the U-boat from taking another shot.

"Sir, *Williams* is launching charges," reported Chief Gunnery Officer Pendleton.

"Very well." He turned to watch as the canisters flew up and over the side of the *Williams*. It was an odd sensation to be nothing more than an observer to the battle, unable to contribute anything to the outcome. He was pleased to feel the ship moving ahead slowly while turning to face the fight directly.

He watched as the depth charges exploded, sending up a small mountain of water that first rose like a giant bubble, then exploded into a shower as it collapsed onto the surface. The objective of a depth charge is to create a shock wave under the water powerful enough to crush the hull of a submarine if the explosion is close enough. Even explosions that did not inflict damage to the sub itself were nerve-wracking to the submarine crew, who had no way of knowing if the ship above them had found them and guessed their depth. The crew of the German submarine had to wait in silence as the ship above them circled and stalked, perhaps ready to launch a second round.

To avoid getting hit, a submarine would often go deep while doing its best to turn away from the attacker. Up top, the destroyer would plot a circle in which the submarine could maneuver, and then the conning officer would make his best guess as to where the sub was heading. With the destroyer's faster speed, they turned inside a circle that would hopefully bring them on an intersecting path with their prey. Sonar often helped in finding the position of the sub, which gave the destroyer captain invaluable information in his maneuvers. But he still had to guess the U-boat's depth to get the charges close enough for a kill.

The telephone talker spoke up. "Captain, Mr. Carroll sends his respects and tells us that he was able to bring twenty Germans on board before we started forward. There are others still in the water that we've left behind."

"Very well." He hesitated. "Tell Mr. Carroll to stand by to take on more prisoners after we're in the clear."

"Aye, aye, sir. Mr. Carroll to stand by."

"Lookouts report no sign of the other U-boat. No indication that the *Williams*'s attack was successful."

Kendrick turned at the sound of Farrell's voice, surprised to have him back on the bridge.

"Good work down below."

"Wish I could take credit, sir, but the chief had things well in hand when I got there. We are taking on water, but the pumps are holding their own. We've managed to seal off enough compartments that we won't sink, barring another attack."

Kendrick nodded. "My guess is that we're in the clear. That other U-boat would be crazy to raise his periscope with the *Williams* so close. From what I can tell, the *Williams* is maneuvering perfectly to keep him down. Of course, only time will tell."

"Aye, sir."

The feeling on the bridge was unlike anything Kendrick had ever experienced. Everyone was tense, as if expecting another blow, but unable to do anything other than watch or tend to their instruments. The usual chatter of idle moments was subdued as people listened as much as watched. Out there was a U-boat that had attacked them and was currently undamaged by the *Williams*. At "ahead slow," with just one propeller turning, they were moving slowly in the water while hopefully reducing their profile to the sub. But at this speed, the U-boat could have easily moved to a different place to get an even better shot. *Or they are moving into positions to attack one of the tankers.* That would be the smart thing to do. It was obvious the *Lester* was severely damaged, so why waste more torpedoes on a useless escort when you could go after the real prize? It was in this moment of thoughtfulness that Kendrick was startled by a report from the crow's nest lookout.

"Torpedoes running! 090 bearing north."

Kendrick looked at the indicated spot in time to see two torpedoes streaking past the *Williams* directly toward one of the merchantmen. "Too late for him," he said in resignation. Two minutes later, two large explosions obscured the merchant vessel in a haze of smoke. "Can you identify the merchantman?" he asked the navigator.

"Yes, sir. It is the *Carnady* carrying wheat and other foodstuffs."

Kendrick acknowledged the report. This was the reason they were here—to protect the convoy, and he was now out of the operation. He saw the *Williams* lurch ahead as it moved in the direction from where the torpedoes were fired. But the destroyer was far enough away that the submarine could take evasive action. Even now, the German U-boat was likely in a crash drive to erase any chance of an easy rendezvous with the *Williams*.

"Sir, report from the *Harker*. They are moving in to pick up survivors." The *Harker* was a small corvette on loan from Britain. With a vessel much smaller than even a destroyer, the crew had their hands full on an ocean crossing with such a small hull to resist the waves. But they were fast, and in this case, they could implement the rescue much sooner than any other ship in the convoy, so he was glad they were so quick to respond.

"Reply to the *Harker*, 'Good work—be quick—be careful!'"

The signalman repeated the message and then moved to send it.

Kendrick scowled in frustration. This new U-boat was proving himself every bit as daring as the one *Lester* had just killed. But the German sub had displayed a folly. It would have been far smarter to have put that torpedo into the *Williams* to force it to break off the attack. With two escorts out of service, the convoy would be fully exposed.

But rumor had it that the senior German submarine officer, Admiral Karl Donitz, was obsessed with tonnage sunk, so he had ordered his U-boat commanders to always go for the ship with the greatest displacement—in this case, the merchant. That was fine, but it left the U-boat still vulnerable to the *Williams*. "But not vulnerable to me," Kendrick said softly. He was trapped on a crippled ship. At this point, he expected that the *Williams* would start a sweep of the area where the U-boat was last known to be and order the *Lester*'s sonar operator to aid in the hunt.

"Sir, would you step out on the wing? Mr. Farrell may have spotted something."

Kendrick acknowledged the messenger and immediately stepped to the outside bridge, where he saw Farrell with his binoculars raised slightly to the port side. "What is it, Henry?"

"There, sir. Just the tiniest of feathers in the water. It's probably nothing, but it could be a periscope just barely breaking the surface." *Feather* was the term used to describe the small froth of water caused by the periscope extending above the surface while under motion.

Kendrick raised his field glasses and looked at the spot. "Hard right turn!" he ordered abruptly. This would be hard to accomplish with a damaged rudder and only the right propeller turning. But he had to act now. Against all odds, the German was not trying to evade the *Williams* but appeared intent on attacking it!

"Mr. Pendleton, swing the port torpedo launcher as far forward as you can and prepare to launch a three-torpedo spread set for shallow, very shallow, and medium." He was flustered, knowing this was not entirely clear.

"Aye, sir. Prepare to launch torpedoes from port, multiple depths!" Pendleton knew exactly what Kendrick was trying for. The chance of torpedoes hitting a submerged U-boat was extremely small because the depth was too hard to gauge. But at the very least, this should scare the wits out of the Germans and perhaps force them to break off their attack on the *Williams*.

Kendrick waited for just a moment as he watched the launching tubes swing forward, then shouted "Fire!" He watched with satisfaction as the first one, then the second, then the third torpedo leapt from the side of the *Lester* and splashed down into the water, leaving a foam trail as the three torpedoes started streaking to a spot forward of where the first officer had seen the feather. While Henry Farrell had been uncertain, Kendrick was confident it was the U-boat, and he had to do what he could to save the *Williams* from being torpedoed. It would be a disaster to have two of three escorts knocked out in the U-boat zone, leaving the convoy almost impossible to protect.

"Signal the *Williams*. Tell them we have launched torpedoes at suspected U-boat position and that they are in line for torpedo attack. They should take evasive action immediately. Send all the coordinates." The signalman acknowledged the order and began transmitting immediately.

Kendrick now reflected on the fact that one of the oddest things about an ocean battle was that once you launched your torpedoes, or depth charges, you had to wait. There was nothing to do but count off the time with a stopwatch, most often to be disappointed when the time to impact lapsed with no explosion. Sometimes you had immediate confirmation of the success or failure of your attack; other times, there was nothing, and you had to slowly relinquish hope and start a new plan of attack on the assumption you had failed.

At this point, it did no good to summon the men to battle stations because they were already there. That meant that all men were awake and at their combat posts, rather than a portion of the crew at rest or off duty. But Kendrick could bring them to full readiness. Stepping to the microphone, he said crisply, "Now hear this. Now hear this! This is the captain speaking. I have reason to believe that the second U-boat is off our port bow, and we are trying to attack them with torpedoes. Not usually a sensible thing to do, but it's our only option. Keep a sharp eye out for torpedoes running toward the ship, and be prepared to move away from the likely point of impact. We cannot muster enough speed to take evasive action. If we are hit, do your duty until we can assess the damage. Good luck!"

Kendrick then stepped back and turned to Farrell. "I'm pretty sure an announcement like that has never been made in the history of the US Navy." Despite the tension, he smiled, as did Farrell.

Then, as they watched the tracks of the torpedoes while counting off the time, Farrell asked, "Why would the U-boat expose itself like that?"

"She was trying to get a shot at the *Williams*. Captain Morrison turned the wrong way and brought himself into her sights. With any luck, the captain of the U-boat was not paying attention to us, having judged that we are out of commission and no longer a threat. There's the slightest chance that we can get him with our torpedoes, although he's likely taking on ballast as fast as his intakes will allow right now since his sonar man has heard our torpedoes running toward them. It's a race to see if he has enough time to dive below our torpedoes."

"Look sharp to port!" shouted one of the lookouts, and to their astonishment, they saw the German U-boat bubbling to the surface.

"What the—" shouted Farrell.

"He heard our torpedoes and judged that he couldn't get down fast enough, so he's surfacing in hopes of the torpedoes running beneath him." There was no concealing the excitement in Kendrick's voice this time. "Mr. Pendleton, bring all guns to bear and fire at will!"

The old *Lester* now had the advantage, since it would take the U-boat crew at least two or three minutes to staff their deck gun and bring it around. He was satisfied to hear the first shots fired from the five-inch guns and watched as the first salvo splashed slightly behind the U-boat. He resisted the temptation to say something to Pendleton, since he was an extremely capable gunnery officer. Kendrick strained to see where the next round of shots would land—hoping it would be right in the main hull of the U-boat, when he was blinded by a massive explosion right midship in the U-boat.

"It's the torpedo!" Farrell shouted. "Our torpedo was shallow enough to get him!"

Kendrick's strategy of three different depth settings had paid off. He knew that the other two would pass harmlessly beneath the German. But that was all right. One direct hit was more than enough to destroy the U-boat.

"Cease fire from the guns!" Kendrick ordered. "But keep a sharp eye in case they try something!"

"Aye, aye, sir," acknowledged Pendleton.

There was no sense in wasting precious five-inch shells. Kendrick pictured the explosion in his mind, imagining what it was like to be on board the U-boat at that moment. Most of the men inside the hull would have been killed by the shockwave of the explosion inside the sealed superstructure. Those who survived would be deafened as the pressure blew out their eardrums. There was simply no scenario in which there was a remaining danger to the *Lester* since the Germans climbing out of the wreckage would be far too dazed by the blast to pose any risk.

"Message from the *Williams*, sir. Captain Morrison sends his regards and says, 'Thank you.'" It was the telephone repeater's job to keep his voice measured so that his words were easy to understand. But in this instance, it was impossible for the pride of the moment not to express itself as the young man repeated the words of the message.

"Tell Captain Morrison, 'Glad to be of help, and please move to shield the convoy.'"

His message was acknowledged.

"Well done, sir!" Farrell said.

Kendrick turned and nodded. "Thanks to your sharp eyes, Henry. A disaster avoided and two U-boats sunk in a single day. That's one for the books."

"Sir, the chief engineer requests that you join him when it is convenient."

Kendrick nodded. "Tell the chief I'll meet him below in five minutes. Mr. Farrell, you have the conn."

"Aye, aye sir." Then to the rest of the bridge party, Farrell said forcefully, "I have the conn." They all understood that to mean that he was now in charge of the bridge as the officer of the deck (OOD) and was the only one authorized to give course changes or operational orders.

Kendrick had a new thought. But, having transferred control, it was not his place to give a new order, so he walked next to Farrell and said quietly, "Henry, it looks like there's smoke at the fantail. My guess is that our right propeller is having trouble. Perhaps you should order all-stop until we get a full report."

"Aye, sir—a very good idea." Farrell then ordered all-stop, which was acknowledged by the lee helmsman. Farrell then said, "Please notify Ensign Carroll to take on additional survivors." Just what Kendrick would have done—and with that, the captain left the bridge.

* * *

Twenty minutes later, Kendrick had the signalman pipe the signal for all hands to listen. After the young man gave the authoritative, "Now hear this. Now hear this!" Kendrick stepped to the microphone, cleared his throat, and said, "This is the captain speaking. All hands prepare to abandon ship. I have ordered the *Williams* to stand by to receive us and the German prisoners we have taken on board. While the ship is presently in no danger of sinking, the damage to the stern makes us unseaworthy. We are simply too far out to make it to port on our own, and it would weaken the defense of the convoy to have one of the other ships tow us. So once all men are clear, the chief and I will scuttle the ship."

He felt the stirring on the bridge but knew sinking it was the right decision. "This will be an orderly evacuation, so be deliberate in your actions." He waited a moment before adding,

"We have done very well today; two U-boats confirmed sunk and just one ship in the convoy destroyed. There are many days left ahead and likely more Germans to attack us, but you have all done your duty. Thank you!"

With that, Kendrick stepped away from the microphone. He was about to send the old *USS Lester* to the bottom of the ocean, and that thought weighed heavily on his mind. Which is why he was so startled when he heard Farrell shout out, "Three cheers for the captain," followed by a boisterous, "Three cheers for the captain—hurrah! Hurrah! Hurrah!" The bridge party was enthusiastic. Even more surprising was that Kendrick heard even louder cheers from all over the ship. Farrell had been at the microphone when he invited the cheers. It was humbling and exhilarating to hear nearly 300 men united in celebrating their achievement. Kendrick was embarrassed to feel himself blush but wise enough to know that the only proper response was to acknowledge the men and then disappear. He nodded to the men nearby and then ducked out the back to make his way down to his cabin, offering a salute to all the men on deck who could see him.

Not such a bad day at sea. There were far more destroyers in the American and British fleet than there were submarines in the German's *Kriegsmarine,* so two submarines for one old destroyer was a profitable trade.

As he made his way below to meet up with the chief, he thought how odd it was that humans often connected emotionally to inanimate objects, like a ship at sea. But now, having spent so much of the voyage resenting the old *Lester* for all it could not do, he felt remorse as he started making plans for how to destroy and sink it. It had, after all, given him the platform to destroy the enemy and had endured the German attacks while protecting the crew. He would miss the *USS Lester*, despite its many flaws.

CHAPTER THREE
A NEW SHIP

February 1944

"THAT'S THE THIRD TIME YOU'VE yawned, John. Late night in Manhattan?"

"What?" Newly appointed first officer John Easton blushed, even though no one could see it. "I mean, excuse me, Captain! I'm awake."

Kendrick laughed. "Oh, don't be so serious, John. A week of shore leave after our sea trials is just what the crew needed. I hope you were out late last night, enjoying a last little bit of sanity before we pick up our convoy in Halifax."

They were standing at the screen of the brand-new Fletcher-class destroyer *USS Warburton* heading north just off the coast of Massachusetts. Receiving command of the *Warburton* in the Atlantic was Kendrick's reward for doing so well with the *Lester*, as well as for his behind-the-scenes work in helping design the Fletcher-class warships. Most of these new ships were being sent to the Pacific, which is why it was considered an honor to have the newest and most powerful destroyer ever deployed under Kendrick's command in the Battle of the Atlantic.

Easton relaxed a bit. This would be his first voyage with Kendrick in command, and he was still getting used to his leadership style. He knew how highly Kendrick valued his previous first officer, Henry Farrell, so Easton felt like he was still on trial in this new role as a first officer, the second-in-command of the ship. Most of the time, Captain Kendrick was relaxed and easygoing, almost to the point of being disconcerting. During the *Warburton*'s sea trials, when practice torpedoes were running toward them, Kendrick had remained calm and deliberate. Even amid the noise and fury of deck guns firing and depth charges exploding, he remained calm. Of course, it would be different in battle, but his new captain's reputation for remaining unflustered preceded him. The captain's calm was far different from the surge of adrenaline that always animated Easton.

I wish I could keep my voice steady, he mused to himself. Easton had also seen action in convoy patrols but so far had not been on a ship that was hit by the Germans, despite some close calls. He hoped he would act rightly if the time ever came.

In response to the captain's earlier question, Easton responded, "As a matter of fact, I *was* out on the town last night. I went to an out-of-the-way little club in Midtown for some drinks with a few of the men I went to Officer Candidate School with. We like to meet there when we are in town. Good live music and lots of cabs to get us safely home after drinking. What about you?"

Kendrick sighed. "I almost hate to tell you because you'll see just how boring and uninteresting a guy I can be. I was at my grandparents' house at a reception. I was the youngest person there and the only one on active duty, so everybody kept asking me how the war was going and all that. As if ours is the only ship fighting. And all that said in front of an admiral and his retinue of hangers-on." Kendrick seemed to catch himself. After a quick cough to mask his embarrassment, he tried to change the subject. "I promise you that you had a lot more fun at your club."

"An admiral?" Easton knew Kendrick had not intended to reveal that detail, but what good was gossip if you didn't pursue it?

"Probably should not have told you that, John. But it's not classified, so I guess it doesn't hurt to talk about it. My grandfather owns a company that supplies communications equipment to the navy—Gatekeeper Electrics. It's a very competitive business right now, so he needs to tend to his political connections. My grandfather's a really good guy who has built up a lot of trust through the years and made a lot of friends. My father, who is now the general manager, thought it would be good for me to be there as window dressing. Fun was not on the agenda."

"Wow!" Easton took a moment to consider this. "So, you're a big shot?"

"I'm a captain of a destroyer in the navy. That's all I've ever wanted to be. My father often browbeats me to resign my commission and come join him at the factory. He complains that now that Grandfather is mostly retired, it is up to him to support everybody financially. It's a tired old argument that lost its appeal ten years ago when I enlisted after graduation."

"Resign your commission? You know, people don't really get to leave the service in the middle of a war."

Kendrick smiled. "What do you think all those political connections are for? My dad, the redoubtable Mr. Vernon Kendrick, tells everybody that he can get me cleared in two days or less because we are classified as an essential war industry. His favorite refrain is always, 'I didn't spend all that money sending you to Harvard, Merrill, just so you'd wind up on an insignificant little tin boat in the Atlantic.'"

He paused. "It's even worse since I spent six months back at Harvard helping develop an engineering curriculum for the new V-12 college officer training program. I was fine doing that for a short while, but my father thought I should stay on indefinitely. He thinks it is prestigious. 'You should either work in the business or in academia but not risk your life on that little boat of yours.'" Merrill dropped his voice and slowed his speech each time he imitated his father. Now he cleared his throat to reduce his irritation.

This was more information than Easton had bargained for. Harvard, an electronics firm, and an escape from the navy anytime Kendrick wanted. There was a lot more to Merrill Kendrick than he could have imagined. "So, if you don't mind my asking, sir, why *are* you on an insignificant little destroyer with all of that going for you?" He quickly added, "Not that I don't think we're a good ship or anything."

A young machinist suddenly interrupted. "Excuse me, sir. But the chief sends his regards and wonders if he could have a word with you?"

Kendrick and Easton turned at the sound of the young machinist mate's voice. It was clear that the young man was nervous just being on the bridge talking to the captain and executive officer.

"Of course, Mr . . ." Kendrick began.

"Soames, sir."

"Of course, Mr. Soames. Tell him I'll be down in a moment."

"Oh, but he's happy to come to you, sir. I didn't mean to imply . . ." Now the young man sounded positively miserable.

Kendrick raised his hand, palm forward. "Not to worry, Mr. Soames. I really need to get down to the engine room anyway. Please tell the chief I'll be there soon."

The young man nodded, saluted smartly, and then turned and left the bridge.

Turning back to Easton, Kendrick said, "John, just let me say this, and then we'll drop this topic. I'll tell you the same thing I tell my father. Gatekeeper Electrics will do just fine with or without me. The V-12 program will be well run by fifty- and sixty-year-old engineers. But if trained officers like you and me don't help Britain win this Battle of the Atlantic, as Churchill calls it, hundreds of millions of people will be forced to live the lives the Nazis impose on them, not the lives they choose to lead.

"Destroyers are small, but they are not insignificant. Right now, we are the best weapon there is at stopping the U-boats from starving Britain and ending the war with the bad guys winning. I know that sounds melodramatic, but it's what I believe. And you and I are among the small handful of officers who know how to pull it off. The battleships and the aircraft carriers are such a tempting target that their officers spend most of their time trying to hide the big ships from the Germans rather than coming out to battle. But we take the war right to the Nazis—we run it right down their throats! And that's what I like doing best—I want to be on the frontline fighting. So, that's why I'm here instead of there."

Kendrick paused to catch his breath. Then he smiled. "Now, see what terrible things you've learned; your captain is both boring and idealistic. What could be worse than that?" Before Easton could say anything, Kendrick put an end to the conversation. "Now, I suggest you order yourself a cup of coffee, extra strong, because I'm going down to see the chief, and then I'm going below to my cabin. You've got the bridge!"

"Yes, sir!" Easton snapped briefly to attention and saluted. He announced to the crew that he had taken over the conn. As Kendrick started to exit the bridge, Easton shook his head. An idealist indeed. He had no idea what that meant for the ship and the crew, but he did know that he would do anything Kendrick asked of him. What could he possibly give up that Kendrick hadn't already given?

* * *

Down below, Kendrick met up with Chief Engineer Bruce Calder. For a moment, Kendrick wondered if all ship engineers were of Scottish descent since all of the chief engineers he had met had similar last names, the same stocky build, and the same kind of no-nonsense personalities.

"Mr. Calder, good to see you. How's the mechanical condition of the ship?" Not the best question in the world, but it was a way to start the conversation.

"You'd think after building twenty or thirty of these Fletchers they'd figure out how to tighten all of the high-pressure rings instead of just most of them."

Kendrick bit his lip so he wouldn't smile. They were standing in the forward engine room—there were two on a Fletcher-class destroyer—and the scale of the machinery was awe inspiring. Two large oil-fired boilers in each engine room reached temperatures of 850 degrees to create 600 pounds of pressure per square inch at the output. The first boiler created the steam; the second turned it into superheated steam; and from there, it flowed through the high-pressure lines that Calder was complaining about to a pair of steam turbines that developed 30,000 horsepower at the propeller. This same process was repeated by the engine room's identical twin on the opposite end of the ship, by the stern, to power the port propeller. Having two separate engine rooms on opposite sides and opposite ends of the ship meant that if one was damaged by a torpedo or shell, the other could still produce power. It was an engineering marvel and far superior to the steam plant of the *Lester*.

"I assume you are getting on top of it."

Calder nodded. "I think we've discovered all the leaks and faulty seals. The sea trials showed us most of the errors of the construction crews." And there it was—the key qualification of an engineer—they always saw what was wrong. That meant they could either fix it or work around it. Kendrick was relieved to have a man of this caliber serving as his chief.

"So, how can I help you?" He almost said "Bruce" but decided they didn't know each other well enough for first names yet.

"Two things, sir. We're having trouble with the torpedo mounts—both sides. I put in a work request back at the shipyard after sea trials, and they were supposed to be fixed, but they still sometimes bind while swinging. I'd like to radio ahead to Halifax to have some of the manufacturer's technical people on hand to assist us. It's not that we can't make our own repairs; it's that they should be part of it, so this doesn't happen again. Plus, there are some specialized parts they could make available that would save me the time of having to fabricate them in our machine shop."

"I'll get right on that. They can fly people up to Halifax if necessary. I think I can pull that one off. What else?"

Calder motioned for them to move out into the passageway. "This one's a little out of my areas of expertise since it has to do with the electronic equipment. I've taken the courses, but I tend to think about large equipment while vacuum tubes and resisters are small and delicate. I'm not really the delicate type."

This time, Kendrick felt comfortable laughing since Calder was obviously making a joke about himself. "Well, who should we talk with then?"

"If you have time, I'd like to take you up to the combat information center to talk with our electronics technician, Able Seaman Holden. He can give you a better understanding of the problem. It has to do with our ship-to-ship radio."

"I have time. Please lead the way." One of the peculiarities of a destroyer was that there were no passages running from front to back. To help keep the ship afloat after an attack, the hull was divided into two distinct sections, and a person had to climb up to the weather deck, exposed to the outside air, in order to cross to the other section where he could go back down into the ship. It was inconvenient, particularly in the middle of a winter Atlantic storm, but it provided additional integrity to the ship in an emergency.

In a few minutes, Calder and Kendrick were standing in the radio room, always hot from the glowing vacuum tubes, which gave off a warm, soothing light that somehow calmed Kendrick. It was one of the things he liked most about visiting his grandfather's factory.

"Mr. Holden," Calder said crisply, "please meet Captain Kendrick."

The young man jumped to attention, almost knocking over his chair as he did so. "Captain!"

Kendrick returned his salute. "At ease, Mr. Holden." The young man widened his stance. "Now, tell me about the problem we're having with the radio."

"Yes, sir. Our shortwave radio is just fine. It's the newest General Electric set, and it's frankly the best one ever made. We should have no trouble with long-distance communication."

"But you're having trouble with ship-to-ship communication, I understand?"

"Yes, sir. It's the newest Gatekeeper model, and I keep having trouble with it. I'll be broadcasting or receiving just fine, and then there will be a burst of static, and I'll lose the transmission. I've been resoldering all the connections, but frankly, sir, it's something of a hazard."

Kendrick drew in his breath, and he hoped the other men did not see his face redden. "That sounds serious. To what do you attribute the problem. Is it a faulty design?"

"No, sir, nothing like that. Gatekeeper has always been one of the best. But it's the construction of this one, sir. It's just not up to military standards. The main components are all okay, but the wiring is sloppy and some of the minor parts, like resistors, are of an inferior grade. When I discovered the problem during sea trials, I ordered triple replacement parts to have on hand, but it could be a real problem in battle when there's no time to make repairs."

Kendrick did his best to keep his voice steady. "Yes, I see that. Do you think it's just this one set?"

"No, sir, I've heard a lot of chatter about it from other ships." Ken Holden's voice turned reflective. "It's surprising because Gatekeeper used to be the gold standard of military radio. They were practically indestructible. But the newest sets are a problem."

Though his thoughts were running fast, Kendrick managed to ask, "What do you suggest we do?"

"If possible, sir, I'd like to replace this set when we get to Halifax. They have an extensive boneyard there from all the ships that pass through, and I'd like to get my hands on either a surplus General Electric, even though it doesn't have quite the range of the

Gatekeeper, or maybe even find an older Gatekeeper model—one that I have more confidence in."

"Sorry, but I haven't heard the term *boneyard* before."

Calder stepped in. "That's what the electronics men call a salvage yard. Mr. Holden is hoping to get his hands on a surplus radio. Oftentimes, they're brand new, just surplus." Calder glared at Holden for using a colloquial term.

Kendrick shook his head to clear his thoughts and calm the sick feeling that had come into his stomach. "Of course. I have no problem with that whatsoever. It never hurts to have redundancy, so taking on an extra set makes sense."

"Oh no, sir, I'm not suggesting a backup. I'd like to replace the Gatekeeper. It's just that I've been in combat before, and every second counts."

"Yes, it does. Thank you for bringing this to my attention. I'll leave it to you and the chief to decide the best course of action. Hopefully, you can find what you are looking for in the Halifax boneyard." He said this in a light tone so that Holden knew he was on solid ground.

"Yes, sir. Thank you, sir!"

With that, Kendrick stepped out of the radio room and motioned for Calder to follow. When he found an isolated spot, he asked, "What about the rest of our equipment—radar, sonar, and internal communication. Is there reason for concern?"

Calder was thoughtful. "I don't believe so, sir. This is the only issue to come up so far. But I'll have the specialists put all the equipment through a round of rigorous testing just to make sure. It's a new ship, so Halifax is our best chance to get things right before heading into harm's way. I'm pretty sure the radio Mr. Holden is referring to is the only Gatekeeper Electrics we have on board, but I'll check on that as well."

"Very good." Kendrick paused. "Thank you for bringing this to my attention. Is there anything else we should discuss?"

"No, sir." Calder hesitated. "I wouldn't normally bring you into a problem like this, but with the ship being new and all, there's sometimes political risk when you single out a manufacturer for criticism. I just didn't want you to get any unexpected blowback when we start rummaging around in Halifax."

"That is very wise of you, Chief. In this specific case, however, I promise that I will manage any blowback. If anything, I'm going to be the one pushing the service about the manufacturer. It is simply unacceptable. So, no worries on your part. Do what you must to make the ship as safe as possible."

"Thank you, sir." With that, Calder saluted and turned away.

Kendrick thought he might throw up. It was obvious that neither young Holden nor Calder had any idea that he was connected to Gatekeeper Electrics. He was relieved that he hadn't said something to tip them off. Even the slightest hint that he was interested in Gatekeeper would have shut down the criticism immediately.

It's my father—he's responsible for this. Now Kendrick found the initial wave of panic being replaced by anger. The fact that Gatekeeper had once been the "gold standard" and was now worthy only to be discarded meant that things had changed—and the only change he could think of was his grandfather's retirement. *So, what am I supposed to do about this?* Kendrick decided he needed to think carefully. He had to take action; but how could he send a message from the ship without alerting Holden or others in the Communications Department about his involvement? He shook his head in disgust and decided to make his way to his private cabin to ponder what could soon be the biggest problem of his life.

CHAPTER FOUR
AN ATLANTIC STORM

JOE HORIUCHI MADE HIS WAY past a group of dockworkers who were busy finishing the re-supply of the steam freighter *Karpa*. Nearly twenty years old, the ship had just completed a re-fit to better prepare it for the Atlantic storm season. As he reached the gangplank, Joe heard under-the-breath comments from those who thought it unjust that a Japanese man could be advanced to the role of chief communications technician, even on an old freighter well past its prime. But that was not Joe's problem. After being rescued from the sinking of the *MaryAnn*, Captain Birdsall had insisted that Joe serve as his communications officer on his next ship. The home office had put up a fight, but Birdsall had enough seniority to force his will on the issue.

Since then, he and Birdsall had made three successful Atlantic voyages together. Aside from some light damage by one German torpedo on their second voyage out, they had made it safely back to the United States all three times. The first cruise was the worst, when the ordinary seamen almost broke out in rebellion at Joe's promotion. They were indignant that someone descended from Japan—America's enemy—could be offered any position. Somehow, they overlooked the many Americans of

German and Italian descent—their native countries also bitter enemies of America—who served actively in all branches of the military, as well as in the Merchant Marine.

Joe knew it was racial prejudice; he looked different, and that's all that was needed. But Joe had faced them down, leaving himself isolated but unharmed. He had considered resigning to avoid the tension but decided that this job was exactly what he had hoped for and that he had earned it. So he endured. Since receiving the promotion, he had done everything possible to serve with excellence.

On the one occasion the ship was damaged, Joe had acted with dispatch to pinpoint the exact spot from where the torpedoes were fired and transmit that information to the military escorts. The naval destroyers had responded immediately and, after a short cat-and-mouse game with the U-boat, had successfully destroyed it with depth charges. The evidence of its demise was a large oil slick that bubbled to the surface, along with clothing and other items floating in the water. The US Navy issued a commendation for Joe's quick thinking and precise reporting, which finally cemented his good standing within the company. He was now considered one of the leading radio men among all those crossing the vast reaches of the ocean. Yet outside his own crew, some still resented him.

"Ready to face the gauntlet again?"

Joe turned at the sound of Birdsall's voice. "It's almost like having an addiction, isn't it, sir? While you're in the middle of it, you think, 'If I get through this, I'll never go to sea again.' But then, when you've been home for a few days, you start to miss the action and are nervous to get back at it."

Birdsall laughed. "I've been told that for something to be addictive, it has to have equal measures of pleasure and pain. I'm not sure what's pleasurable about going to sea in the middle of a war, but the pain is certainly obvious."

"The pleasure is perverse—the adrenaline rush that comes from danger." Joe thought for a moment. "And from knowing that we're doing something worthwhile with risks that few others are willing to take."

By this point in the war, they had become close friends. Jim Birdsall was a philosopher with an engineer's touch while Joe was an engineer who enjoyed the occasional discussion of philosophy. They'd spent hours talking with each other on their previous journeys—to the point that the rest of the crew had finally left Joe alone. It was as if he had entered a new class all his own—not an equal to whites but not someone to be despised like others of his race. He was just Joe, the communications guy and friend of the captain. If anything, his slightly elevated status came at Birdsall's expense since it diminished his standing with the crew. But Birdsall did not seem to care.

"Well then, let's make our way to Halifax to join a convoy," Birdsall said. "I'm told this one will have a beefier escort than any of the crossings we've been on before. Apparently, the navy has a new class of destroyer that can run circles around a submarine. And with any luck, we'll be positioned right in the center of a convoy, as far away from harm as possible."

Joe swallowed hard. He hadn't heard about this before. He leaned close to Birdsall and said quietly, "In other words, we're carrying ammunition!"

"Ammunition, field artillery, and land vehicles with fuel tanks full of gasoline."

Joe shook his head. "Well, at least it will be over quickly if we do get torpedoed. Few survivors ever get off an exploding ammunition ship."

"We will go out in a blaze of glory! If the *Karpa* explodes with all that we're carrying, we'll light up the ocean, and they'll see the column of fire on both sides of the Atlantic."

Joe did not fully understand why Birdsall was so cavalier, but it did calm him. "Well, now the adrenaline is kicking in, so I guess it's time to feed our addiction."

Birdsall laughed, and the two men made their way up the gangplank.

* * *

"Everything all right, Captain?"

Kendrick glanced away from his first officer before responding to him. He knew that the bridge crew had noticed his subdued demeanor, but he was having trouble putting on a relaxed face. The phone call he had made from Halifax to his father was simply too frustrating to get past. "It's none of your business" was the essence of his father's reply, with a few added expletives. But he could tell that his accusation had rattled his father—as well it should. If Vernon Kendrick *was* taking shortcuts on government contracts, he could go to prison. And worse, men at sea would die. Merrill could not imagine why this was happening.

He shook his head. His first officer had just asked him a question, and yet his mind was going back into the depressing replay loop that he often encountered after talking with his father. It was pointless yet inescapable.

But now was not the time, so the captain of the *USS Warburton* squared his shoulders—he had to step into the role of a ship's captain, unafraid and undisturbed by anything. Leadership often required a person to become an actor assuming a confident persona on the outside that they may not yet feel on the inside. *Get it together, Merrill,* he thought to himself. Then he turned to face Easton squarely.

"Everything is fine, John. I have a lot on my mind is all. What can you tell me about our provisioning?" This was another trick he had learned from one of his early captains—the best way to deflect attention was to ask a question.

"We are well stocked, sir, including the special items you requested and paid for. I hope it's not out of line to say that you have excellent taste in food and drink." This was a risk on Easton's part, but he clearly hoped to draw the captain into conversation.

Kendrick nodded and forced a smile. "It's a small thing that I'm happy to share with everyone in the officers' mess. With all the irritations we put up with at sea, having decent chow is a small indulgence that can have a positive effect on morale." He paused, then gave a genuine smile. "At least, it improves mine!"

Easton was pleased to see the captain relax his shoulders. Perhaps his gambit had paid off in calming his captain down from whatever it was that was bothering him.

"Believe me, sir, we appreciate it. I won't ask how you get all of this despite the rationing at home. Just know that we are grateful."

"No cheating on the ration list. All of this is legitimate. It does help to play the 'We're out there on the ocean helping defeat the enemy' card when negotiating with suppliers." He nodded thoughtfully. "And a willingness to pay top price, I suppose." This time, they both laughed.

Since the days of sailing, it fell to officers to pay for their own food, and the best captains often purchased premium products to gain loyalty from their officers. It was something of a recruiting tactic back in the days when captains had to assemble their own wardroom. "And we are topping off our fuel supply right now. We should be ready to sail at 0500 as ordered."

"Very good." Kendrick was successfully back in control of himself. The problems at Gatekeeper Electrics would have to wait until they returned to New York. Now they were in Halifax about to lead the largest convoy yet, and that should be his only concern for now. "Thank you, John."

"For what, sir?"

Kendrick knew Easton had purposely started this needless conversation for the express purpose of bringing him into the present. But he could not say that. "For getting all the arrangements just right. Yours really is the hardest job on the ship—you manage everything behind the scenes while the captain makes the 'executive decisions.' Just know that you are doing the job well, and I appreciate it."

"Thank you, sir." Easton was furious that he had blushed at this compliment. He really hadn't been fishing for one, and he hoped that the captain didn't think that he had been brown-nosing. That was a new phrase that was disgusting both in the image it created and in what it meant. He did not want it to apply to him.

"Don't overthink it, John. You really are doing well. I've been there myself. The first officer is responsible for everything, including complaints, but gets none of the credit. That is why there is a little surprise for you in your bunk when you go off duty. I hope you enjoy it."

"A surprise?" Easton laughed because it was not usual for a captain to create a surprise.

"Just my way of saying thanks. Probably the last time I'll think to say it, so again, I hope you enjoy it."

"Thank you, sir. Now I'm curious."

"And yet it will be hours before you find time to get down there. So, I have given you the even greater gift of anticipation. I hope you enjoy that too." Then, before Easton could respond, Kendrick said firmly, for all to hear, "I'll be off, then, Mr. Easton. Lots of paperwork to complete, and I've got to get ready for our dinner with the merchant ship and escort captains at 2000. Got to give them as much confidence as possible before we sail out into the storm." To everyone on the bridge he added, "Mr. Easton has the conn!" With that, he turned and exited the bridge.

* * *

Joe Horiuchi swooned. Never had he been seasick on all his previous voyages, at least, not throw-up-over-the-side-until-you-wish-you-were-dead seasick. But this current North Atlantic spring storm was about to bring that record to an end.

"How does the ship survive this?" he asked desperately as the *Karpa* shuddered from crashing into a sixty-foot-high wave. It seemed impossible that the steel could stand the impact. The bow was first crushed under a thousand tons of water as the giant wave crashed down on the deck, then lifted as the trailing end of the wave raised the bow. This left the bow suspended high in the air for a few moments as the wave passed under the length of the ship, simultaneously lifting and dropping different sections as it did so. The groaning of the metal as it responded to this longitudinal caterpillar of compression and tension made the ship sound like it was a giant beast trapped in a medieval torture chamber.

"Worst I've ever encountered," Jim Birdsall said complacently. "I'm glad we have a full cargo hold or we'd capsize for sure."

Joe desperately tried to force his stomach to remain calm but recognized at the last possible moment that his stomach wasn't listening to his brain just now, and so he grabbed the garbage can underneath his radio desk and finally let go. He hated the convulsions as he wretched up everything he had eaten in the previous twenty-four hours. When the spasms finally subsided, he grabbed a towel to wipe the sick off his face and then another to wipe the sweat from his forehead.

"That will help a lot . . ."

Joe was not in the mood to be consoled, even by his only friend on board. But even in the depths of the greatest misery he had ever experienced, he was wise enough not to snap back. So he settled for, "I hope so because I need help right now. I've never been this sick in my life."

Birdsall pulled up a chair and sat down beside him. "You're not going to believe me, Mr. Horiuchi, when I tell you this. But you need to eat some soda crackers. Food will actually calm your stomach."

Joe simply groaned at this advice. His head was spinning, and he knew that if he lived through the storm, he would never eat anything again, let alone some soggy saltine crackers. While he said nothing, his intent was obvious.

"Suit yourself," Jim Birdsall said evenly. "But I've been through this before. Some people are sick for up to three days after their first bout of seasickness, and the truth is I can't have you out of action for that long. I need you at the radio now more than ever, since we're steaming in the middle of more than forty ships who are all being thrown off course by this weather. You must make this work!"

Joe looked up and then reached out his hand to take a handful of the dry crackers Birdsall offered him. "Has there ever been a mutiny because the captain tried to kill his crew with crackers?"

Birdsall laughed. "I'm not sure it will provide any comfort, but you have to know that it's far worse for our friends on the escort ships. We have 10,000 tons plus cargo to stabilize us in the water. Even that new Fletcher-class ship, the *Warburton*, is only 2,100 tons. With their sharp bow, they knife so far into an approaching wave that it's nearly up to the superstructure before they bob their way up to the surface. Their up-and-down motion is far greater than ours. I bet they're holding on for dear life right now."

"Then they all deserve medals for not committing suicide," Joe said miserably. He wasn't usually so negative. But the nausea of motion sickness is unlike any other malady that afflicts the human body and mind—precisely because it affects both. It starts with a conflict between the motion detected by fluid in the inner ear and the relative stability of being inside a steel canister where the objects at hand seem stable in their relative position according to the eye. A person's ears say they're moving, the eyes say they're not, and the brain doesn't know what to make of it—so it panics. Without its "place and position monitors" working together as usual, it concludes that it must have been poisoned (another cause of nausea) so the beleaguered brain initiates the purge response of throwing up. Soon both the brain and body are involved, leading to a uniquely disorienting kind of misery unlike any other.

"Are you all right, then, Joe? I must check on the rest of the ship, but I need someone at the radio who is ready to sound an alert the moment something comes through. Should I send someone to relieve you?"

Joe shook his head—an exquisitely painful thing to do, as it turned out. "I will make this work, sir!" Joe felt that the conversation had turned from friendly to formal with Birdsall's last question. "The crackers actually are helping, although I'd have bet my entire college fund that they would make it worse." He swallowed carefully. "So, I'll be all right."

"Darn it. I wish you'd have offered me that bet. I could have taken your college fund and turned it into my retirement fund," Birdsall said. Joe was relieved their conversation had become friendly again. "Well, you call me if you think you need help. Your job is even more important right now than usual."

"Thank you, sir. I'll be ready for whatever comes."

Birdsall stood up and left. Joe earnestly hoped that he could keep his promise because, right now, all he could think about was reaching for the garbage can again.

* * *

"I'm ready to receive your readiness report, Doc Carver. I hope you have some good news," Kendrick said. *Doc* was an honorary title bestowed on all chief medical corpsman on a ship, even though few had been through medical school, while their assistants were called pharmacist mates.

Chief Medical Corpsman Daniel Carver saluted. "Right now I wish I *was* a doctor, sir. We have over thirty percent of the crew on the disabled list, and frankly, I'd say that one hundred percent are at least slightly impaired. Being seasick is worse than being drunk, you know? Just maintaining equilibrium uses up an enormous amount of mental energy."

"Thank you, Mr. Carver." Kendrick didn't like to interrupt people, but his medical officer tended to go on and on about things. "But what exactly does it mean for thirty percent to be on the disabled list? Are they completely out of action?" It was difficult for Kendrick, who had never experienced seasickness, to have empathy for those who were sick. He thought it a moral failing on their part, as if they should simply will it away through concentration.

Fortunately, Carver knew this about the captain. He had served with him on the *Lester* and knew him to be kind and compassionate about nearly everything—except seasickness. "I've been very conservative in only listing those who are so severely impaired that they honestly can't function in their stations. Naturally, they would take up battle stations if we came under attack, but doing so imperils the safety of the ship since their response times are so slowed by the nausea."

He struggled to think of a way to explain it. "Think of it like this, sir—you are able to conn the ship because of the mental map you maintain inside your head, which is constantly updated with time, position, and speed. Isn't that true?" When Kendrick nodded, Doc went on. "You are able to do this because of fluid in your ears that responds to changes in motion—something like the spinning of the ship's gyroscopes. As long as all the elements move in the proper relationship to each other, they give an accurate reading.

"But suppose that someone came and gave the gyroscope a fierce jolt, knocking it out of alignment. It can no longer orient itself properly. That is what seasickness is—the parts of the body that convey place and motion become desynchronized. Just imagine putting a gunner into place and asking him to fire on an enemy target when he can't properly assess up and down or side to side. How could he ever sight the gun?"

Easton watched as Kendrick inhaled sharply. Easton had experienced several waves of nausea himself since the storm began more than twenty-four hours earlier. But he was fortunate that he adapted quickly, and for the moment, he was reasonably clearheaded. What he couldn't assess was whether the captain would take offense at Carver's analogy.

"I have to tell you, Mr. Carver, that I honestly don't understand. But I do trust your judgment. I've seen the men stagger as they make their way to railing." Kendrick inhaled again slowly, then let the breath out even more slowly. "The problem is that the U-boats enjoy an enormous advantage over us. They can submerge a hundred feet and miss the effects of the storm entirely. When they are forced to rise to the surface to take on new air and recharge the batteries with their diesels, they may encounter problems, but by and large, they can ride out the storm safely submerged. So, they are in full fighting trim while we're up here getting seasick." The disgust and dismay were clear in his voice.

Carver hesitated, then said quietly, "I do have one potential solution available, sir, although it is unproven at this point."

Kendrick tilted his head. "Do tell me more, Mr. Carver!"

"While on leave in New York, I attended several medical conferences at the base and was told about a new experimental drug called scopolamine that, given in small doses, has been shown to reduce motion sickness in most patients. The side effects are drowsiness and dry mouth, but most of the patients in the study thought it well worthwhile. Because of my interest, the medical officer in charge offered me some samples that I could give to any of the men who volunteer."

Kendrick was about to respond when he checked himself. Part of the reason for the check was that a particularly violent wave crashed over the bow, causing the ship to stutter in its forward motion for a moment. Everyone on the bridge simply swayed in response and quickly regained their footing. But the main reason for his check was to get more information and see what his first officer thought of the idea.

"What do you think, Mr. Easton? Do we give the men an experimental drug that could affect their judgment but that holds the promise of relieving their motion sickness? Is it worth the trade-offs?"

Easton was firm in his response. "I say give it to any man who wants it. They are already miserable and already impaired. I don't see how it can make things worse, and we'll benefit from any improvement."

"Do you believe it's worthwhile, Mr. Carver?"

"I do, Captain. I won't give it to anyone who doesn't want it, and I'll monitor it carefully to stop future administrations if it causes any problems."

"Very well. Make it so. Thank you for your help. I appreciate it when someone brings me both a problem and a potential solution." He saluted, and Carver withdrew. Turning to Easton, Kendrick said, "This really is unfortunate, John. The convoy is in shambles, and the other escorts are as bad off as we are. We must keep the watertight doors sealed, so we can't use the lookouts or other deck crew to keep us prepared for action."

"I'd think it would be difficult for the U-boats to launch an attack in these storms. I don't see how they could properly launch torpedoes with the seas so devilishly high."

Kendrick nodded. "I'm sure you're right. Our biggest problem is potential collisions within the convoy columns. I wish I knew how long this damnable storm will continue." He swaggered as the ship jerked yet again. "Come smartly into the waves!" he said firmly to the helmsmen.

The last wave hit them at an angle, which was something to be desperately avoided since a wave of this size hitting them from the beam could potentially swamp the ship.

"Come smartly into the waves, sir!" The helmsmen were earning their pay during these shifts, with constant adjustments required to keep the ship on course and into the waves in a storm such as this.

"Very good." He waited a moment and then added, "And a very good job at that!" Fortunately, they were on a four-hour-on and four-hour-off routine, so the men standing at the wheel had time to recover from the strain.

"John, I'm going to the communications shack to reach out to other ships to try to figure out how far we have drifted off course. There is no sense in maintaining radio silence right now, and I want to know as much as I can. You have the conn."

"Yes, sir!" Then to the rest of the bridge crew, Easton said crisply, "First Officer has the conn." He knew it was going to be a very long night.

* * *

"Captain Birdsall!" Joe shouted urgently into the ship's interphone system. "I think we've got a problem!"

Birdsall was on his handset in an instant. "What is it, Mr. Horiuchi?"

"The *Warburton* has been collecting relative positions of all ships in the convoy, and the *Ellenberg* oil tanker just reported theirs. If they are right about where they are, then we are on a collision course with contact at any moment!"

Jim Birdsall's mind swirled. "Are they in front of us or behind us? How should I react to avoid a collision?"

"In front of us. Here is the position they reported." He then repeated the coordinates through the interphone. Unlike most of the radio operators, he had been keeping notes on all the reported positions so that he could build his own map of the convoy. It was this map and his meticulous attention to the *Karpa*'s own position that led him to see the danger. But he did not know enough about how a ship operates to find a solution. Fortunately, he heard Captain Birdsall shout to the helmsman, "Hard to port," and then to the lee helmsman, "All ahead slow!" Even with his inexperience, Joe knew this was a very dangerous command with the seas running this high. The turn to port would expose their flank to the waves, and the command to slow the ship would reduce their maneuverability.

"Dear God, I hope I got this right," Joe said to himself. He was startled when he heard Birdsall reply through the intercom.

"I hope to the dear Lord that you got it right as well—if not, you might be meeting Him much earlier than you expected!"

Joe was dumbstruck that even in a situation like this, Jim Birdsall could find time to be witty. Joe was convinced that's why Birdsall had survived so long against the odds. Joe also resolved to keep his thoughts in his mind, rather than saying them into a microphone.

The result of Birdsall's commands was immediately felt. As the ship turned to port, they were hit broadside by a huge wave that sent a shudder the entire length of the ship. Joe found himself sitting on the floor where he had been thrown from his chair.

"Oh my—"

The next thing he heard, though, was not the sound of the ocean but the screeching-tearing sound of metal on metal! It was like a thousand fingers dragging themselves down a chalkboard, and he covered his ears to mute the sound. Having just stood up from being thrown out of his chair by the wave, he now found himself flailing forward as two mighty ships crashed against each other. How was it that fate would cause the two largest ships in the convoy to find each other rather than either meeting a smaller ship that would do less damage? As Joe crashed into the wall, he had the bizarre experience of remembering a story about how, in 1895, there were only two cars in the state of Ohio, and they managed to crash into each other. He did not know if it was true, but right now he could certainly believe it.

Overhead, the Klaxon horn sounded, summoning all crew members to general quarters. Joe picked himself up, anchored his chair to the floor, and then took up position at the radio while awaiting instructions from the bridge. It was disconcerting to hear and feel the two ships jostling against each other, and he wondered if a spark caused by the collision had started a fire somewhere on the ship. *Not a good thing on an ammunition ship*, he thought.

Finally, he heard Birdsall's voice in his headset. "Horiuchi, send out a distress signal to the commodore and to the *Warburton*. Tell them that we have minor damage with some leakage on the starboard side, but it's nothing the pumps can't control. Be as brief as possible and let them know we are moving away from the tanker. And be sure to give them our new position."

"Aye, sir—" Joe started to say, but Birdsall had already broken the connection. Joe felt a flood of relief wash over him. They had collided, but side-to-side rather than with the bow of the *Karpa* slicing into the tanker. It was bad but not nearly as bad as it could have been. He quickly sent the message as instructed and then waited. And waited. Then he checked his set to see if it was functioning; the *Warburton* was always quick to respond.

He swore. On checking the set, he could see that one of the vacuum tubes was dark instead of glowing. "It's this new Gatekeeper. What a waste of wires this thing is." He quickly pulled the top off of the cabinet, disconnected the power, then set about adjusting the tube in its socket. Just to make sure, he tipped the set up on its side—not an easy thing to do with the jumping of the ship—and determined that a solder connection had come loose. As fast as possible, he heated his soldering iron and fixed the problem. Then he turned the power on, not waiting to replace the cover, and urgently sent the message again. This time, there was a quick reply from *Warburton* indicating that they should move ahead as quickly as possible to avoid being hit by a ship behind them in the convoy.

The advantage of being in the middle of the convoy was that it offered protection from submarines. But in a situation like this, their position increased the number of ships that could crash into them. Joe quickly repeated the information to Birdsall, who took immediate action to comply. The *Karpa* was damaged but serviceable. Joe wondered if the same was true of the tanker, but he knew better than to interrupt the men on the bridge to find out. It was comforting when he felt the engines come throbbing to life, and he felt the ship shudder as it turned once again into the waves. The old pounding and bucking started up again. Just an hour earlier, he had hated that sound and motion. Now it felt wonderful.

He shook his head as something dawned on him. "I'm not seasick!" In the heat of the moment, he had gained his sea legs.

CHAPTER FIVE
FIRE IN THE WATER

"Any word from the commodore?"

Commodore was an honorary title given to the merchant marine leader of a convoy. He was often a retired naval officer who was not yet ready to leave the ocean. His job was to keep the cargo and tanker ships in proper position relative to each other as the convoy snaked its way across the Atlantic to Britain. It was not an easy job, given that these ships had wildly varying speed and maneuverability and particularly since the group was often forced to respect radio silence to prevent the Germans from triangulating their position. And though the commodore was the leader, he was always subject to direction from the escort group commander, who was an officer in the US Navy.

"Just that at least two submarines have been spotted, and the escorts are moving to intercept," Joe said in a flat voice. "Now that the storm has eased, they expect activity to pick up with the increasing visibility."

"We'll be receiving orders to disperse in a few minutes, which means we'll be more vulnerable than ever." Jim Birdsall's voice was *not* flat when he said this. As the ships in the convoy fanned out to provide more distance between individual ships, it would become easier for a submarine to move in to attack the ships in the center of the formation. The Germans assumed that those were the highest-value targets since they had the most protection. It was as if the *Karpa* had a giant bullseye painted on it.

Joe reported to Birdsall, "A new message from the *Warburton* indicating that a third U-boat has been spotted on the northern side of the convoy."

At this point, radio silence was no longer necessary since the Germans clearly knew where they were and had assembled a wolf pack to intercept them. A wolf pack was just what it sounded like—a pack of hunters assembled to kill as many Allied ships as possible. Defending against it was a formidable challenge since a U-boat could pop up in one location, fire torpedoes into the convoy, then disappear under the waves. The surface escorts would then change course to attack the sub, which drew them away from other parts of the convoy, creating a new opening for another U-boat to attack there. Even with four destroyers and five corvettes, it would be almost impossible to protect all forty of the cargo ships, thus making it almost a certainty that death would take a toll on the ocean this day.

At this point, Birdsall had returned to the radio room to check up on Joe. "Who knew that we'd come to miss the storm so quickly," he said. The weather had cleared, they had stabilized the light damage to the hull from the collision, and Birdsall had even remembered to thank Joe for his quick warning. "But why did it take the *Warburton* so long to respond to our distress call?" he asked.

This prompted Joe to offer his unflattering opinion of the new Gatekeeper longwave radio set. "I wish I had brought some old sets along to rebuild so I could throw this thing into the ocean." But since being appointed communications officer, he had not had time to work on old radios, so he was left with the Gatekeeper.

Birdsall started to say something, but Joe held up his hand. "Message coming through from the commodore: all ships to disperse to pattern A-14."

"Thanks!" Birdsall was off, racing to the plot table to refresh his memory of this pattern and give the orders to assume their new place in the line. Once they were executed, he addressed the crew: "All hands, this is the Captain! The convoy is under attack by at least three U-boats, with more likely to show up. We've just been ordered to disperse, which means we'll be more difficult for the U-boats to find. We are faster than they are when submerged, but this also means it will be easier for them to draw a bead on us. So, all hands not needed below deck should move to their assigned observation posts. It is urgent that you report any torpedo tracks or even suspected tracks the moment they come into view. We are running at full speed ahead, so we will have some maneuverability. Quick action may prevent disaster." For a moment, he paused. "Men, this is a time for courage! The very act of signing up for this ship shows that you are brave and dauntless, and I have great confidence in you. Do your duty and keep a sharp eye!"

With that, he switched off the intercom. Turning to his helmsman, Birdsall said, "It feels good to be going full speed, although I don't know how long we can maintain it and still have the fuel we need to make it to England."

Always a quick wit, the helmsman replied, "We can always siphon the gasoline from the military vehicles. I was really good at that in high school!"

Birdsall laughed and patted the fellow on the shoulder.

* * *

"Sir, ops reports that another merchant ship has been hit in the northwest quadrant."

"Very well." Kendrick did not think it appropriate to say, "Very good," in such a circumstance, but he needed to acknowledge the report with something. "Five ships torpedoed, three down and two sinking." He did not expect a reply from Easton.

"But we have reason to believe two of the U-boats have been sunk."

Kendrick was amused—no, not amused exactly. He admired that Easton always tried to put a positive spin on things. Kendrick tended toward the negative.

"And I'm going to get the one we're chasing or die trying!" Kendrick's nostrils flared.

Easton nodded. He had come to believe that Captain Kendrick was very much like a cat in pursuit of its prey. Once a cat decided to kill, it became hyper-focused until it struck. Kendrick had been pursuing this specific U-boat for more than an hour. Each time its periscope popped up to get a bearing on a merchant ship, Kendrick was after it. Still, it had somehow managed to launch two torpedoes into a lumbering merchant ship that sank in less than ten minutes. That had infuriated everyone on the bridge. In the heat of battle, it was hard to feel despair for those who died—that would come later—but for now, they felt anger that all their efforts had failed to protect the ship under their watch.

All they could do now was try again, so they followed the track of the torpedo back to its origin and moved immediately to intercept the U-boat, unleashing several tons of explosives to rain down on it from above. The hardest part was guessing the depth; it was not so difficult to locate the horizontal position using sonar and sightings. But how deep the U-boat would dive was always a guess. Easton could not imagine that they had missed it on their last run and even rejoiced when an oil slick rose to the surface—but Kendrick was convinced the slick was a decoy, a trick used by submariners to make a pursuing surface ship think the U-boat had been sunk when, in reality, it had just released oil to float to the surface while the sub was still safe under the water.

"Stay on it," he urged the sonar and hydrophone teams. Sure enough, after a ten-minute wait, they discovered that the U-boat had kept still in the water and was now moving toward the center of the convoy.

"Come to course 0350," Kendrick ordered. That would take them ever so slightly west of almost due north and right into the middle of the convoy. It would also make it tricky to avoid the merchant ships, so Easton ordered an extra set of lookouts specifically for that purpose.

"Ease to course 0290," Kendrick added, a move that had them sailing west amidst a convoy sailing east.

It made Easton dizzy to think how Kendrick could keep track of all the other escort ships while simultaneously conning the *Warburton* for an attack on the submarine they were chasing.

"Mr. Easton, I need to check on the other escorts. Will you please hold this course for ten minutes and then brief me if we've reestablished sonar?"

"Yes, sir." He took control of the bridge while Kendrick moved to his ready room just off the bridge to communicate with the other escorts. With so many U-boats circling, it was essential that they coordinate their attacks as much as possible.

* * *

While Joe Horiuchi loved his job, he did regret that it kept him isolated in a windowless room behind the bridge. He sometimes yearned to look out onto the ocean. This desire was particularly acute when they were under attack, since he had no idea if a torpedo was headed their way until word came over the intercom.

"I guess it would be worse to be in the engine room, below the waterline." He shook his head irritably at the thought that he was talking out loud to himself again. But it sounded good to hear a human voice in the open air, rather than through the radio headset, so he continued. "I'm not sure I could do it—I've never had claustrophobia, but to be down there in the hold knowing that you are in the direct line of fire—wow!" He shuddered at the thought. What was even worse was that the men who were in the engine room were surrounded by high-pressure boilers, high-pressure steam lines, and an insane amount of flammable liquids and lubricants. It was counterintuitive to think that many men were burned to death at sea, even as several tons of ocean water flooded into their compartment. "Okay, I'm glad that I'm up here instead of down there. I'll stop complaining!"

He still wished he had a window.

His reverie was interrupted by the radio. "*Karpa! Alert!*"

He acknowledged the hail.

"Warburton *reports U-boat moving toward center of the convoy. They are in pursuit. Execute zigzag pattern within your assigned parameter. And keep an eye out for* Warburton *to offer them room to maneuver.*"

Joe quickly relayed this to Birdsall, who acknowledged the command. Joe immediately felt the ship turn to port to initiate a new zigzag pattern. The goal of the zigzag was to be unpredictable so that a U-boat sighting in would have difficulty getting a precise firing solution for their torpedoes. Since it took several minutes for a torpedo to travel from the attacking submarine to the intended victim, an unexpected zig or zag could turn them away from danger . . . or into it.

"Anything else, Mr. Horiuchi?"

Joe shook his head at this. Was Birdsall questioning if he passed along all the information? Joe felt his indignation rising but then took a deep breath to calm himself. He was sure that no offense was intended—it was just Birdsall's way of dealing with anxiety. "That was the full message, sir. No follow-up offered."

Birdsall's silence told Joe that the captain had realized his mistake in challenging Joe and was embarrassed by it.

For the next thirty minutes, Joe listened to the short clips of chatter that went back and forth between the commodore, the escorts, and the other ships in the squadron. To tamp down his nerves, he updated his plot of where each of the ships in the column had moved to, as well as marking a large X wherever one of the ships had been torpedoed. There were now six, making this a particularly deadly encounter. He cheered when one of the escorts reported the destruction of a third U-boat.

Birdsall walked past his radio shack just as Joe cheered, so of course he stepped back in to ask what had happened. When Joe told him about the U-boat, Birdsall replied, "Seven to three doesn't sound so good, until you realize that there are nearly 3,000 ships in the Merchant Marine and fewer than 100 U-boats at sea at any given time. So, the loss of three is a greater problem for Germany than seven is for the Allies."

"Unless you're one of the crew of the seven . . ." Joe said quietly.

"Yes, unless you are on one of the boats that gets hit. It doesn't make the papers, but I saw a confidential company report that shows the Merchant Marine is suffering a higher casualty rate than any of the military branches. We are the slow-moving ducks that Germany has to kill to win the war."

Joe had never heard Birdsall talk like this, and it disturbed him. "Are you all right, sir?"

"The U-boat that the *Warburton* is chasing is coming for us, Joe. Don't ask me how I know—I just know it. They've passed up too many opportunities to fire on other ships farther out in the grid. And we can't zigzag fast enough to defeat their firing solution if the *Warburton* allows them to get a periscope sighting on us."

Joe started to challenge this—after all, the U-boat may have been forced to stay down by the relentless pursuit of the *Warburton*—but he decided against it. Birdsall did not need arguments; he needed support. "What can we do, sir?"

Birdsall turned and looked at Joe. Then an expression of resolve came over his face. "That is a very good question, Mr. Horiuchi. While there's precious little we can do to prevent an attack, what we can do is prepare ourselves to save the crew if we do get hit. If they hit us in the forward hold, then most of us are done for because the ammunition will go up in flames. But a hit anywhere else gives us a few precious minutes . . ." His voice faded. "Thank you, Joe. I know what I need to do now."

And with that, he left.

Joe wondered what he had possibly done to help.

* * *

Captain Kendrick rubbed the back of his neck for perhaps the two hundredth time since this battle had begun. It was now more than twelve hours since the first convoy ship had been sunk, and they were rapidly approaching sundown. That would make it even easier for the U-boats to attack. He wished he knew how many were still out there, besides the one he had now lost. "Any word from either radar or sonar?" This was not a specific request because Kendrick knew he would be notified just as soon as a reliable contact was made, but it was something to say.

"The most recent report is that the U-boat must be near the surface because sonar can't get a reading with all the other ship hulls in the area, and radar hasn't detected anything like a periscope."

Kendrick thanked the officer of the desk (the OOD). Radar was only effective within 1,500 yards of the target, and there was too much noise from all the ships in the convoy for the hydrophone operators to hear anything distinguishable.

Tedious minutes passed. Then the messenger, an ensign, spoke up. "Sir, radar indicates a possible periscope or tower at 0350, range 1,000."

Kendrick felt a surge of much-needed adrenaline. "Very good."

With just those few words, the atmosphere on the bridge transformed itself.

"I'll take the conn," Kendrick said to the OOD.

"Yes, sir. Captain has the conn!"

"Do any of the lookouts have a visual?"

"There, sir!" said a young ensign who was in rotation to be on the bridge.

Kendrick followed his outstretched arm, stepped to the open platform, and lifted his glasses. Sure enough, there was a slight feather in the water, although it was difficult to see with the sun behind it.

"All ahead flank speed!" He then gave new coordinates that would point the bow of the *Warburton* just ahead of the U-boat, if that's what it was.

"All ahead flank speed!" the lee helmsman confirmed. It was impossible for the man to disguise the excitement in his voice.

"I think he's trying to attack the *Karpa*!" Easton said urgently and very close to Kendrick's ear.

After jumping at the sound, Kendrick turned to Easton. "And the *Karpa* is carrying a full load of munitions and other field equipment. If they go up, it will be quite a sight, to say nothing of the shrapnel endangering any nearby ships."

"Yes, sir. *Karpa* is the ammunition ship."

Kendrick felt his stomach lurch. "By the way, welcome back to the bridge, John. You are remarkably stealthy in your ability to appear at my elbow at just the right time."

"Sorry, sir. Didn't mean to startle you."

"I'm glad you're here."

The messenger spoke up, "Sir, radar reports they've lost contact."

"Very well." Then, "It makes sense. He's getting ready to fire his torpedoes."

"And what are our intentions?" Easton asked, trying to be heard above the noise of the ship lurching through the water at almost thirty knots.

"I'm going to ram him! Our deck guns are no use, and there's no time to get off torpedoes. Would you go to the intercom and alert everyone to brace themselves?"

"Yes, sir!"

Kendrick registered that Easton looked astonished, but he didn't have time to think about it. "You are so focused, *Herr Kapitänleutnant*, on shooting the *Karpa* that you aren't paying attention to me," Kendrick murmured to himself. "You figured there was time to get your torpedoes off, then dive and force me into the old pattern."

"Sir, sonar reports target dead ahead, 200 yards and closing rapidly."

"It has to be more rapid than this," Kendrick said as he moved to the communications board. "Chief, if you have any miracles in your pocket, pull them out now. I need more speed, and I need it in the next twenty seconds but for just a couple of minutes!"

"Aye, sir," Chief Holden replied sardonically. "I'll be off to throw some kerosene in the boilers."

He wouldn't really do it, but Kendrick knew that the chief would allow the steam pressure to climb just a little past the high-danger mark on the pressure gauge. Sure enough, in a moment, he felt a slight lurch as the ship gained even more speed.

"Sir, underwater search detail reports torpedoes in the water."

"Very well!" Then he shouted up to the lookouts, "Torpedoes running—tell me which way they're headed!"

It took a few moments before they reported back that they could see a trail in the water heading perpendicular to the *Warburton*, which meant the Germans had fired on the munitions ship.

"Signals, notify the—what was the name of the ship—the *Karpa* that they are under attack."

The order was confirmed, and he turned to watch, expecting to see the ship start evasive action. But it held to its course.

Kendrick swore loudly. "Send the signal again. Use the light if you need to!"

This, too, was confirmed, but as far as he could tell, the now-doomed ship was doing nothing to protect itself.

"Brace for impact!" He had watched the U-boat from the moment the periscope had gone down, done the mental math in his head as to distance and speed, and concluded that even if the U-boat had now initiated a crash dive, the *Warburton* ought to at least hit their conning tower. "Assuming all my calculations are correct," he said to himself.

With no visible sign on the surface, he had to estimate when the impact would occur, and he was shocked when it didn't.

He swore again.

But he was even more shocked when, five seconds later, he was thrown forward against the railing with such force that he felt himself lifted up and off his feet, putting him in danger of toppling over the front of the grating. Grabbing hold for dear life, he felt some hands grabbing him from behind—Easton, of course.

"I think you got him, sir," Easton said casually.

The sound of the two vessels crunching against each other was horrifying, and Kendrick hoped against hope that he hadn't torn a gash in the bow of the *Warburton*. Then, just as quickly as it started, the sound of metal ripping against metal disappeared, which meant that with their forward momentum, they had fully crossed over the U-boat.

"All ahead slow!"

"All ahead slow!" Within a few moments, the ship slowed quickly in the water.

The next thing to happen was a large explosion off the port side. "A torpedo struck the *Karpa*!" one of the lookouts shouted.

Kendrick turned in that direction but shielded his eyes in anticipation of the munitions exploding. He was surprised to see that the ship was still afloat, rather than exploded into a billion pieces.

"The torpedo must have hit a non-critical area," Kendrick said, relieved. "Ensign Porter, assemble a team to search for survivors. But be careful, Ensign—if there are fires onboard that ship, it could explode at any moment. So don't go in too close."

The ensign nearest him acknowledged the order and moved to assemble a rescue crew.

"Damage report?" he asked Easton, who had moved to his emergency station to begin receiving reports from all over the ship. In what seemed like an eternity, but was probably just two minutes, Easton finally reported the very good news that the hull had not been breached, although there was noticeable damage to the bow. "They build them well in Brooklyn," Kendrick said triumphantly, and Easton returned his smile.

"Doc reports that other than a few broken bones and several hundred bruises from men falling forward, there were no casualties," Easton said.

Kendrick shook his head in disbelief. It had gone as well as could be hoped for. "Okay, now find out about the U-boat."

It was a complicated task with three ships in play, especially with one that might yet explode. He turned to the OOD, who reported that there had been a massive release of bubbles to the surface as the ship passed over the U-boat, and now there was debris floating to the surface, but no survivors.

Kendrick thought for a moment. "Probably not surprising. If they were initiating a crash dive, they would have pressurized the hull. Our collision would have caused all that air to explode upward, likely killing most of the crew as it did. And then, with the conning tower torn off, the ship would have quickly filled with water." Kendrick shook his head—not in regret, but perhaps in respect. Anywhere from thirty to fifty men had just lost their lives in service to their country, and that was a sobering thought.

The radio operator spoke up. "Captain, a distress call has been received from the *Karpa*. And on the northeast quadrant, the *Williams* reports that they have lost contact with the U-boat they were chasing but that it was definitely on a course *away* from the convoy."

"Very good. Tell Captain Morrison to break off the attack and start reassembling the convoy. And tell him thanks for his good work today."

"Yes, sir!"

Kendrick was glad that Morrison was again with him on patrol. He was now a highly experienced U-boat hunter and had likely saved hundreds of lives that day.

Now, what to do about the *Karpa*?

CHAPTER SIX
DEATH IN THE WATER

Things were not as bad on the *Karpa* as they could have been. After his last conversation with Joe Horiuchi, Captain Birdsall had ordered all non-essential crew to move to positions on the outside decks so they could make a quick escape if torpedoed. When the lookouts finally spotted the torpedoes in the water, Birdsall immediately ordered "abandon ship" in advance of the collision so that the men in the engine room could start making their way to their assigned emergency station. He could always call them back if the torpedoes missed, but with four torpedoes in the water, the chances of a miss were slim. In perhaps the luckiest break of the day, only one of the four had hit, and it was at the stern of the ship—away from the munitions loaded in the bow.

Had the *Karpa* been a regular cargo ship, with food or non-explosive war material, Birdsall would have stayed on board to see if they could salvage the ship. But with fires in the stern, it was inevitable that sparks and heat would work their way through the ventilation systems to the forward hold, and the risk of an explosion was simply too high. Hence the abandon-ship order.

Birdsall reached the lifeboat at the same time Joe did. "I think the *Warburton* was trying to warn us about the torpedoes, but that new radio garbled the transmission. We could have had another two or three minutes to take evasive action!" Joe's voice conveyed his fury.

"Fortunately," Birdsall replied, "they signaled with their lamp at just the last moment so that I could start a turn to port to narrow our profile. That's why we were struck in the stern instead of at midships!"

By now, the lifeboat was in the water, and they started rowing furiously in the direction of the *Warburton*, hoping the destroyer would take time for a rescue.

"It's an odd feeling to be leaving a ship that isn't in immediate danger of sinking," Birdsall said.

Joe was about to respond when the whole world went incandescent. It felt like the skin was being ripped from his face. As the leading edge of a shockwave blasted over them, he was lifted and hurled out of the lifeboat, literally flying through the air. The concussion left him gasping for air, and soon Joe Horiuchi faded into unconsciousness.

* * *

"Ensign, I see another one over there! Portside."

Ensign Porter strained in the dimming light of sunset to see the object his crewmate had spotted. "Got it! But is it debris or a person?"

"Can't tell. But it's the size of a person."

"Let's go!"

With that, the crew of the rescue boat strained against the oars. The rescuers had just been lowered into the water when the *Karpa* exploded. There was a small, initial concussion, followed by a second that was eardrum-shattering. Fortunately, most of the men had been looking down at their oars so they avoided being blinded by the flash from the explosion. Even so, this particular rescue boat was thrown against the hull of the *Warburton* when the blast hit them, but it did not tear apart. Two rescuers were temporarily blinded, and two others had their shoulders crushed when they were thrown against the destroyer. These men were quickly replaced, and then the various rescue boats were sent out in the direction of the wreckage as soon as the subsidiary explosions subsided.

So far, this crew had pulled just three men from the water. A second rescue boat had also lifted some men, but Ensign Porter did not know how many. Most of the *Karpa*'s lifeboats were blasted into splinters with all onboard men killed. But some had been thrown clear and were still clinging to life. "Why, it's a Japanese or Chinese guy!" Porter said in surprise.

"Is he alive?" a rower asked.

Porter reached over the side as they drew near. "I don't know. He's not moving. But his head is up and out of the water because of his lifejacket."

"If he's not alive, we should just leave him," an ordinary seaman said. "Why should we rescue a Japanese? They're the enemy."

"Not so fast." Porter was young, and it was a constant struggle for an ensign to manage a crew of older men, but Porter was no pushover. "Give me a minute." Porter put his wet index finger under Joe Horiuchi's nose and watched a small bubble form. "He's alive. Help me haul him in."

Some of the men turned away, which aggravated Porter, but those closest to him reached down and helped him lift Joe by the lifejacket up and over the side of the boat. Joe came sloshing down in the center, toward the bow. When some of the men recoiled, Porter said harshly, "Knock it off! He's just a man who has been hurt, and he poses no danger to any of you! And he's serving on an American ship, so he's probably an American." He expected some blowback, but instead, his words seemed to increase his status with the men. "Okay, does anybody see anything else?"

It was hard to tease survivors' bodies out from the pieces of the wreckage. The *Karpa* had been blown to pieces from multiple explosions, and there was no ship left to indicate the position of where survivors might be.

Finally, an older seaman said, "Mr. Porter, we can keep looking, but these men are in urgent need of medical attention. Perhaps we ought to get them back to the ship?" He posed it as a question so that Porter could give the order without appearing weak.

"You're right. Thank you." Then he gave the command to return to the ship. There were some young officers who would not have given credit or expressed appreciation, but this crew did not see it as a weakness, and Ensign Porter returned to the ship as a newly accepted member of the crew.

* * *

One of the young officers assisting Kendrick glanced down at the side of the ship and then reported, "That's the last boat coming in now, sir—Ensign Porter's boat, I think."

"Thank you." Kendrick kneeled and put his hand under the neck of the broken body that was wearing a captain's uniform. He glanced up at Carver, who shook his head. This man was dying. "Is there anything I can do for you, Mr. Birdsall?"

Birdsall tried to shake his head, but it was too much effort. Then he rallied. "There is one thing . . ." Kendrick leaned closer to him to hear, recognizing the effort it took for the man to speak. "If they rescue a man named Horiuchi—he's Japanese—will you watch out for him? He's a genius when it comes to radio and electronics." Birdsall coughed, and Kendrick tried to help him straighten his throat. "And . . . and he's my friend. He has a tough time of it being Asian, but he's a good man and can be very helpful. I made him my chief communications officer. Will you watch out for him?"

"I promise I will."

Birdsall shifted uncomfortably, and Kendrick let his head settle on a pillow that Doc had provided. "There must be something you can do," he said to Doc Carver.

"I can give him an extra-large dose of morphine. In addition to having multiple broken bones and a collapsed sternum, he's covered in burns. I'm sure he must be in agony."

"Then do it!" Kendrick stood up. "Have you seen a Japanese survivor?" he asked Carver, who shook his head in the negative.

Easton spoke up. "I think Ensign Porter may have rescued him." He motioned to the siderail, where a limp body was being brought on board. Kendrick moved in that direction, waving for Carver to follow him.

"Is he alive?" Kendrick asked Ensign Porter.

"Yes, sir. But he has been unconscious the whole time. I think he has some bad burns, but I don't know what else is wrong."

Kendrick looked up and saw several men staring at the limp figure who was being lifted onto a stretcher. He also saw that a number had declined to help. He started to say something but checked himself. *Pick your battles carefully*, he thought. But to let everyone know exactly where he stood, he walked over to the stretcher and motioned the loitering seamen away so that he could help carry the man down to the infirmary. That caused a stir, but he was confident it would give some protection to the man if he regained consciousness. As Kendrick looked down at him, it seemed a remote possibility. Once he and the other fellow reached the stairs, two ordinary seamen stepped forward and asked if they could take over. Kendrick was surprised at how much this gesture moved him, and he quickly said thank you and allowed them to take his place.

"Take good care of him, Doc. I made a promise to the captain, you know."

"I will. It was his dying request."

Kendrick turned quickly to where Birdsall had lain, and he recoiled when he saw the pharmacist's mate draw the blanket up and over the captain's face.

"Germans!" Kendrick swore. Then the captain turned to all the men in the staging area who were helping the handful of survivors and motioned for their attention. When all had turned his way, he said with just enough force to be heard, "Good work from all of you. This was hazardous duty, and you performed well. These survivors owe their lives to you. Thank you for doing your duty."

He then turned and made his way to the bridge, where he gave the command for the ship to move forward to take its place in the screen. As he glanced through the reports from the other escort ships and from the commodore, he concluded that this attack had been repelled with the loss of seven ships. That was an appalling toll. But they had three confirmed U-boat kills and a possible fourth. So that was good. It was harder for the Nazis to build U-boats than it was for the Allies to build cargo ships. Brutal math, but relevant.

* * *

"Time to breathe at least a small sigh of relief," Captain Kendrick said.

"Yes, sir. The last ship of the convoy is in range of land-based aircraft. The odds of a U-boat attack go down considerably from this point forward."

This was one of the best moments on an Atlantic convoy—when long-range aircraft from the British Isles added air cover to an incoming convoy. These aircraft could often spot a submarine from the air and either attack it directly or provide its coordinates to the regular convoy escorts so they could move in for an attack. The Germans had an extraordinarily high casualty rate for U-boats within this protected range and so had backed off on their attacks within this zone, which was a great boost to convoy success in contrast to the early days of the war when the approaches to the English ports was the most profitable U-boat hunting ground. After all, there was a lot of ocean for a convoy to hide out in when in the middle of the Atlantic. When the lines had to converge down to just a few ports equipped to handle the ships as they arrived, the U-boats could hide nearby and then launch their attacks. But now, with both air cover and an ever-increasing number of destroyers, it was dangerous ground for both the hunted and the hunters.

"With respect, sir, Doc Carver wonders if you could join him in the infirmary at your earliest convenience," a young midshipman said to Kendrick.

"Very good. Please tell Mr. Carver that I'll be down shortly."

The young midshipman saluted, and Kendrick returned his salute.

"I'll be leaving you, then, John." Kendrick did not have to turn over the conn because he had never taken it from the OOD. He reserved that privilege for battle situations. Otherwise, it left his mind clear to have the OOD keeping track of the routine maneuvers of the ship while he stayed connected to the other escorts. First Officer Easton acknowledged his command and indicated that he was going below as well. As the executive officer, he had to check on all departments of the ship to assure continual readiness. He turned the conn over to a senior lieutenant, and then he and Kendrick left the bridge. When they were gone, the remaining bridge party breathed a sigh of relief.

* * *

"How can I help you, Mr. Carver?" Kendrick seldom called him Doc, even though it was appropriate to do so.

"Ah, Captain. I thought you'd like to meet Mr. Horiuchi. He regained consciousness a few hours ago, then slipped back out. But I think he is waking up again. I've had to give him quite a lot of morphine for pain."

"Thank you. I do want to meet him." Kendrick started toward Joe, but Carver put a hand on his arm.

"Before you do, I think I should update you on his medical condition. I'm afraid Mr. Horiuchi is going to discover a painful new reality."

"What do you mean?"

"His left leg was severely injured by the explosion. I had to amputate just below his knee to prevent gangrene from setting in. And I'm not sure how much use he'll get from his left arm. Right now, it fails to respond to stimulus. My guess is that he'll get back some use of it, but he's likely to have permanent damage."

Kendrick sighed. He would be among the casualty statistics, which listed both wounded and killed. "Those with permanent disabilities have paid a high price for their service," he said to Carver. "Thank you for helping all these men. I know it's rather overwhelming."

"I wish I were a doctor so I could do even more. But we managed to save seven men. Out of a crew of fifty, that's not many, but it matters to them."

"It's fortunate we weren't closer to that ship when it exploded. The lee helmsman reported that he watched a piece of their bridge launch more than half a mile into the sea. We got hit by some shrapnel but no injuries."

Carver corrected him gently. "We did get some bleeding eardrums from the blast. And a lot of the men continue to complain about ringing in the ear. It's a condition called tinnitus, and it's likely to last a lifetime. It means diminished hearing at certain frequencies, as well as the annoyance of 'hearing' a phantom, high-pitched whistle at the frequency where hearing was destroyed."

"I may have some of that myself. I couldn't believe the force and sound of that explosion." Kendrick shook his head subconsciously, then realized that he had done that a lot since the explosion. "I've been in battle many times but have never experienced anything like that."

"Do you want me to look in your ears, Captain? I'm not sure what I can do to help."

"No, I'm okay. Others have it much worse. And now I can pretend not to hear people when I don't want to talk with them." He smiled. "Now, will you introduce to me Mr. Horiuchi? I don't even know his first name."

"Yes, sir." With that, Carver guided him to the bed, where a very disoriented Joe Horiuchi was trying to raise his left arm.

"Mr. Horiuchi, this is Captain Merrill Kendrick of the *USS Warburton*. He's been asking about you, so I thought the two of you should meet." He turned to Kendrick. "Captain, according to his dog tags, this is Able Seaman Joseph Horiuchi, Merchant Marine, formerly of the *Karpa*."

Joe tried to straighten up, but Kendrick put a hand on his shoulder to calm him. "It's all right. Rest easy."

"Pleased to meet you, sir," Joe said awkwardly.

"And I'm pleased to meet you. How are you feeling?"

This agitated Joe, who started shifting in the bed. "I don't know what's happened to my arm. And I can't feel my left leg. Can you tell me what's happening?"

Kendrick took a deep breath. "Our medical officer has given me some news about your condition, and I'm afraid you'll be disappointed." He then proceeded to deliver the grim news of Horiuchi's leg and arm. He braced for Horiuchi's reaction but was surprised when he responded simply that he "had suspected as much."

"I know I've been out of it for several days, but during the more recent times when I did regain consciousness, I could feel pressure below my knee." He paused and swallowed hard. "So, I had an idea this had happened."

"I'm sorry." Kendrick had learned that the best response was to be honest and straightforward. He felt bad for this man and that "sorry" was all he could offer.

"May I ask you about the captain of our ship—Jim Birdsall? Did he survive? Is he all right?"

"I'm afraid not," Kendrick replied quietly. "His injuries were too serious. But he did talk with me before he died. And of all the things he could choose to talk about, he asked me to watch out for you and make sure you're all right. It was the last thought on his mind."

Joe caught his breath and worked to suppress a sob.

Kendrick put his hand on Joe's uninjured right hand. "He told me that you were friends and that I would do well to use your many talents."

Joe drew a deep breath. "He was my friend, the only one I had, really . . ." His voice trailed off.

"I'd like to learn more about that and about your skills with respect to electronics. He said you're a genius."

Joe lifted his lower lip. "That's just how he talked."

"Well, I do want to learn more. But I think you should rest now, and I need to get back to my duties. But will you promise that we can talk in more detail soon?"

"Yes, sir." Joe struggled again to control his emotion. "Thank you, sir. And thank you for being with Mr. Birdsall at the last. He was much more than men judged him to be."

"I believe that's so," Kendrick said softly as he watched Horiuchi close his eyes to sink back into the world of dreams. Turning to Carver, Kendrick asked, "What's next for Mr. Horiuchi?"

"We'll get him to a hospital in England where they can do a proper job of stitching up his leg. We need to get his bone shaped and skin grafted to form a healthy stump—one with little or no pain and that is free from infection. He will then have to make a choice as to whether he wants to live with a partial leg, using crutches to get around, or be fitted with a prosthetic leg. Of course, that might be out of his reach . . ."

"Why wouldn't he choose an artificial limb? That must be easier than using crutches and not as noticeable."

Carver looked at the captain quizzically. "You do realize, sir, that the prosthetics that a common seaman in the Merchant Marine can afford are not high quality. They are difficult to manage and painful to wear. It is very taxing on a person. Crutches are more predictable and far less expensive."

"This is new to me. Are there high-quality devices that are more functional and comfortable? It seems to me that with his injured left arm, crutches might also be a challenge for Horiuchi."

"Ah, yes—hadn't thought of that. To answer your question, there are profound differences based on a person's ability to pay. The very best devices are custom fitted to the stump—I'm sorry to be so graphic—so that there's a firm connection to the tibia to provide stability. But even with the best, it's still awkward and takes time for a person to become proficient."

Kendrick was thoughtful. "What is your schedule like while we're in England? We're likely to have a four-week turnaround to make repairs."

"I don't really have plans, sir. I've never been there, so I was hoping to get a transfer to London just to see the place. But otherwise, I'll work on restocking the infirmary."

Kendrick nodded. "I'll see that you get to London. But I wonder if you would take special care with Mr. Horiuchi, assisting him through the surgery and then helping him select an artificial leg of the highest quality."

"But, sir, I thought I explained—"

"This is where I need complete confidentiality. I will pay for the new limb, but I do not want him to know about it. Perhaps you can say that you have access to a charity that will cover the cost. At any rate, I'd like him to have the best possible." Kendrick had not looked directly at Carver until this point, when he raised his head and looked at his eyes.

"That's very generous, sir."

Kendrick shook his head slowly. "This man has so many challenges already. Just being Japanese in this service is hard enough. He also just lost his best friend and supporter, so now he'll be even more vulnerable." He pursed his lips. "This is really a very small act to give him some hope. Can I count on you to be discrete?"

Carver nodded. "Actually, sir, this is a good opportunity for me as well. I've always been fascinated by war injuries and prosthetics. I had an uncle who was injured in the last World War, and his artificial arm was frightening to me as a child until I got to know him better. Then I came to appreciate the huge sacrifice he had made by his military service. I will be happy to help Mr. Horiuchi with this. It's kind of you to make such an offer."

"No one else can know—not anyone!"

"You can trust me, sir. I'll let you know what develops."

CHAPTER SEVEN

AN AWKWARD DINNER
IN NEW YORK

THOUGH CALLED KENDRICK AT SEA, he was Merrill at home with his family. A formal dinner with his parents and grandparents was never a relaxed event, but this one was extra tense with Joe Horiuchi as Merrill's invited guest. It was bad enough that his parents were uncomfortable with Joe being there, but when Merrill glanced at their server, Evans, and motioned for him to refill Horiuchi's glass, he was irritated to see Evans narrow his eyes as he reluctantly stepped forward to serve Joe. Evans clearly thought it an affront to his dignity to have to serve someone of Asian descent.

But Merrill was not the only one comfortable having a Japanese man sharing a dinner with the family that evening. As far as Merrill could tell, his grandfather was fine with Joseph being there. He had employed men like Joe for many years and was comfortable with them, regardless of their ethnic background. Of course, Merrill had cleared it with his grandfather before inviting Joe. Merrill's father, Vernon, was indifferent to Joe's ethnicity, though a bit offended that a "laborer" would share their dinner. He had earlier whispered, "It is probably all right to meet him, Merrill, since Joe is a veteran and shipmate of yours, but it would have been better if we'd met somewhere discrete for drinks rather than here for dinner."

Merrill Kendrick's mother was the most put off, likely out of fear that neighbors on the street would learn of it. In her mind, it simply was not acceptable to have any "Orientals" join them for dinner, even worse knowing that he was Japanese, given the concentration camps that West Coast Japanese had been sent to. Merrill had no idea what his grandmother thought, as she was both too kind and too polite to make her thoughts known on an issue of an invited guest once the event had started.

Yet, Joe was here, at Merrill's invitation. Merrill's only regret was that Horiuchi looked miserable. He had not wanted to come, but Merrill had insisted, telling him that it was necessary for a job that he hoped would open to Joe.

What Merrill had not told anyone was that he was really staging an ambush—a trap to ensnare his father, Vernon. He was sure the evening would turn ugly before long. Even Joe didn't know; he would likely clam up if he knew Merrill's true intentions. Merrill had come up with this plan after talking with Joe in England and learning why the *Karpa* had failed to respond to the *Warburton's* radio message about incoming torpedoes. Joe had told him about the malfunctioning Gatekeeper radio, but Merrill had not told him of his own connection to the manufacturer.

Now that both Joe and Merrill were back in New York City, Merrill was determined to confront Gatekeeper's problems, and he knew that if he had given anyone an advance warning of what he was intending, his father would have gone to work to thwart it—by cancelling the party or other means. Or Joe might have refused to come to the dinner, and his story was crucial to the confrontation. It was even important that Merrill's mother and grandmother be present so they understood the gravity of what Vernon was doing—after all, they could exert influence on the company as well. So, Merrill pressed forward in what was sure to be an awkward evening for them all.

As the servants stepped forward to change plates for the next course, Merrill spoke up, doing his best to sound relaxed and conversational. "Joe here is something of a prodigy when it comes to electronics. In fact, he attended Rensselaer Polytechnic. He was chief communications officer on his merchant ship before it was sunk by a German U-boat in battle."

This had exactly the effect he hoped for. His grandfather, Edgar, perked up, and his father motioned for one of the servers to step forward to light a cigarette. It was considered gauche to smoke during a meal, but Vernon was so addicted that he could not wait until after supper. It was also Vernon's way of signaling his complete lack of interest in the topic.

"Rensselaer—that's a fine school. What did you study there?" Edgar's voice conveyed his real interest in asking the question.

Joe was so self-conscious that he stammered. "Uh, mostly radio, sir. Though I'm interested in all types of electronics. Anything that can be amplified."

"Radio . . ."

Merrill interrupted his grandfather, knowing that he was about to mention Gatekeeper. "As it turns out, it is possible that Joe's ship might have been saved but for the failure of the ship's radio. Perhaps you could tell us about that, Joe. Both my grandfather and father are interested in radio technology, as it turns out."

"Your radio failed?" Edgar asked urgently.

"I'm not sure this is the right place—"

"Yes," said Merrill's mother. "Perhaps dinner is not the best place for such a conversation . . ."

"No, please tell us," Merrill pushed. "I want everyone to hear it." He looked to his grandfather, who nodded his agreement.

"Well, it's just that the set was very unreliable. It would intermittently stop receiving the signal, and at the height of that final battle, I did not receive a crucial transmission from Captain Kendrick's destroyer that was trying to warn us of approaching torpedoes. If we'd have received the message, we might have taken evasive action sooner."

"I agree with Mr. Horiuchi; we do *not* need to discuss this at dinner," Vernon said emphatically.

But Edgar had already started talking and did not stop because of Vernon's interruption. "Intermittent—how is such a thing possible? Military standards are so rigid. I can't see how a radio could possibly fail. Had it been damaged prior to the battle?"

"No, sir," Joe said with a little more confidence. "It was a problem right from the beginning. I tried to resolder all the contact points because many had cold solders that cracked. But some of the resistors and other components were simply inferior grade. I'd have swapped the radio out if I'd had time to find anything better."

Merrill cast a quick glance at his father and saw that he was smoldering. While Edgar was in a problem-solving mode with no idea what was coming, Vernon had sensed that there was danger.

"I need to step out to finish this smoke," Vernon said.

"What make was the radio?" Merrill asked forcefully.

"Why, a Gatekeeper. I thought we'd talked about that, sir."

Edgar nearly fell over backwards. "Gatekeeper!"

The two women looked stricken.

Vernon cursed, caught himself, and then said, "For the love of Pete, Merrill, is that what this dinner is all about? Did you bring this man here to tell us that his radio is why he's all blown up like this? What kind of a thing is that to do in front of your mother and your grandmother? If you've got a problem with me, why don't you come straight to me with it?"

At the intensity of this reaction, Joe pushed himself back from the table. "What did I say?"

Merrill was about to respond to his father but was preempted by Edgar, who asked urgently, "Are you telling me, Mr. Horiuchi, that a Gatekeeper Electrics radio had defective parts in it and that it failed at a critical moment while in battle?"

"Father, this isn't the time or place—"

But Edgar shushed Vernon.

Joe looked at Merrill, then glanced at Vernon and back to Merrill, who motioned for him to answer. "I have no idea what I just said, but the answer is yes. Gatekeeper used to be the most reliable brand in the world, as far as I'm concerned. But lately, they have been substandard. I don't know what other word to use for it." He was clearly embarrassed but also angry that simply telling his story had caused such a stir. "I don't know why that's a problem for you, but it sure is a problem for everybody who has one of the new sets. Mine wasn't the only one."

Vernon was standing now. "I will not sit here and listen to this." And he refused to sit back down even when Edgar told him to. "I'm leaving! These histrionics are tiresome and insulting!"

After Vernon had stormed out of the room, Merrill motioned to his mother and grandmother to stay where they were.

His mother shook her head. "Oh, Merrill, why would you do this to your father?"

If he could have stood easily, Joe would have done so. Merrill rose and stood behind Joe's chair and then rested his hands on Joe's shoulders to reassure him. "It's all right, Joe. I'm afraid I had to find a dramatic way to emphasize an alarm I've been trying to raise with my father and grandfather for some time now."

Joe looked up, confused and angry. "But what has that got to do with me?"

"I am the founder of Gatekeeper Electrics," Edgar said quietly. "My son is the current general manager. We own the company that made your defective radio." Edgar looked up at Merrill. "And my grandson has been trying to tell me that the company has been taking shortcuts under my son's leadership—something I haven't wanted to listen to."

"Oh my . . . How can this be happening?" Joe said quietly. He now shifted his shoulders so that Merrill removed his hands. "You shouldn't have done this to me, Captain Kendrick. That's not right."

"I'm sorry, Joe. But I had to do something. I couldn't get through any other way."

"But why at dinner, Merrill?" his mother asked. "Why did you need to embarrass all of us, including Mr. Horiuchi? And how can you be certain that your father is responsible?"

"Because, Mother, you'll notice that father blustered about it, but he did not deny that he *is* responsible. The fact is that he is responsible, and we should all be embarrassed and humiliated. Father has been taking shortcuts—ordering his staff to use inferior components as substitutes—so we can sit in splendor while men are dying out there." He looked fiercely around the room. "We are all part of this, and we need to do something right now to fix it!"

Before anyone could respond, he motioned to Evans to bring Joe's coat, which Evans did promptly.

"I'm going to take Joe back to his hotel now. I know this was a terrible thing to do to you, Joe, and I'm sorry for that. But nothing else I have done or said has had any effect. Now maybe we can do something to make things right at the company."

Edgar stood and walked over to Joe, who stood up awkwardly. He motioned for his crutch, which he used in combination with his new leg. It was clear that everyone in the room, except Edgar, was angry. Edgar was abashed, embarrassed, and sick to his stomach at the realization that men at sea were at this moment in danger because of Gatekeeper Electrics.

"Mr. Horiuchi," Edgar said, "I am so sorry for what happened to you on that ship. I am heartbroken to think that my company had anything to do with it. I hope you will forgive me enough to talk to me about this in more detail. I need to know as much as possible about the problems with your set. Perhaps I can visit you at your hotel or you can come to our factory."

Joe was speechless. "Yes," he said at last in a quiet voice. "I suppose I could do that. I'm sorry to have embarrassed you."

Edgar shook his head, making it clear that Joe was not at fault. "As for you, Merrill, you've finally made your point. I should have listened much sooner. Will you come back and talk to me? I may need your help."

"Yes, sir. I will." Merrill's voice had lost its edge. He turned to his mother and grandmother. "I hope you'll excuse me—for everything." Neither said anything, but his grandmother put her lips together in a way that indicated she understood. Then, as he started to help Joe toward the door, she came around the table and stepped in front of Joe.

"Thank you for coming, Mr. Horiuchi." She reached down and took his free hands in hers. "I don't know much about what you've been through, but I'm sorry for it. And I hope that someday you will come back to our house. You will be welcome."

"Thank you." Joe could only shake his head.

As they stepped through the door, Merrill motioned to his chauffeur to help him with Joe. "Did you see where my father went?"

Richard motioned to the left. "He walked down the street that way, sir. He looked upset."

Merrill nodded. "He should be." Then again, more quietly, "He should be."

* * *

"Captain, welcome to the ship!"

Kendrick saluted his first officer. "Sorry I haven't been more help, John. I have several off-base problems I'm working on. What is the status of the ship?"

"Repairs are on track, our ammunition and torpedoes have been loaded, and our victuals should arrive tomorrow. As of right now, we are on schedule to depart on Friday."

Kendrick gave a sweeping glance over the main deck of the *Warburton*. "Very well. Thank you for taking care of everything. What about the crew?"

This was a persistent problem on all ships in port, not just military ships. Crewmembers granted leave often overstayed or overdrank, and rounding them up was a chore.

"Fortunately, our new quartermaster, Edward Drake, is a compulsive fellow, and he seems to be tracking the movements of every single crewmember. I'm confident that we'll have the highest attendance in the port."

Kendrick laughed. "That is a big load off your shoulders. If our Mr. Drake has been following my movements, he is likely a little bit crazy by now. I've been from Cambridge down to Baltimore, and I'm not done yet."

"With respect, sir, you don't really have an understanding of the phrase 'rest and relaxation,' do you?"

Kendrick laughed again. After their previous voyage to England and back, along with the shore time in England while repairs were made on the *Warburton*, he had gained a genuine appreciation for Easton's droll sense of humor.

"Well, they say an idle mind is the devil's playhouse, and so far, he has had little claim on me. Which brings me to another point. I should be coming onboard now, but I have some nasty business to complete this afternoon and maybe tomorrow. Is it all right if I show up at the last minute on Friday?"

"Yes, sir. Of course. You know from your own time as first officer that it's a dream come true not to have a captain fussing around while you're busy. No offense intended." Easton hoped this would be received well.

"None taken." Kendrick stirred uneasily, his thoughts fractured in a dozen ways. In the past two weeks, he had created the confrontation at his grandfather's, gone to Harvard to review the curriculum for leadership training, been in Maryland to discuss design considerations for newer Fletcher-class destroyers based on the *Warburton*'s experience in recent battles, and met up with Joe Horiuchi a number of times—alongside Kendrick's grandfather— to discuss both the longwave and shortwave radio sets. He had also been to the Gatekeeper factory, where production standards had already been improved with heightened oversight from his grandfather. His father had been obdurate, acting very annoyed that Edgar had reinserted himself into the business. Now, Merrill was off for what was sure to be a momentous discussion about the future of the company with officials of the War Department. It was a meeting he did not want to attend, which was likely the reason for his stalling at the *Warburton*.

"You said you had an important meeting?" Easton tried to sound casual, but Kendrick knew instantly that Easton wished Kendrick would leave the ship.

So, he laughed a third time. "I'm leaving; I'm leaving!"

As he reached for his hat, Easton said quietly, "I'm not sure where you are off to, but good luck, sir. It must be awfully important."

"Thank you, John. It is. Perhaps we can talk about it once we are out at sea. In the meantime, please keep up the good work. I appreciate it."

As Kendrick made his way to the gangplank, Easton rubbed his chin thoughtfully. It seemed that there was no end to the depth of this captain. He hoped that he could help clear Kendrick's mind once they were at sea. Having lots of irons in lots of fires made for an interesting life, but in battle, one needed just one iron in a deadly fire.

* * *

"Are we waiting for the general manager of Gatekeeper Electrics, or should we begin?"

The War Department supervisor who was meeting with them held a civilian grade equal to that of a colonel in the army, so Washington had sent someone with command authority. Merrill's anxiety had risen sharply when he and Edgar entered the bland little conference room in a nondescript federal office building in lower Manhattan where he found not one, but five federal authorities in attendance, including one representative each from the US Navy, US Marine Corps, and US Army. It was all right to have so many involved, since Gatekeeper sold radio sets to all branches of the military, but he had hoped they could start out more quietly.

"Our general manager, Vernon Kendrick, will not be joining us today," Edgar Kendrick said.

"Well, Mr. Kendrick, you requested this meeting. Tell us why we are here."

Edgar cleared his throat. Over the course of many decades, he'd had hundreds of meetings with government employees, but none like this. "Yes, well. I asked you to join us so that we can alert you to a significant problem with Gatekeeper field radios that have been deployed in each of your services. I'm afraid that we have had quality control issues that have made a number of models unreliable. I have anecdotal proof of sets failing even in battle. As you can imagine, this is my worst nightmare and something that we want to correct as soon as we can. But to do so, we'll need your cooperation."

The chief inspector, a fierce-looking man named Bernard Colby, raised an eyebrow. "And just what is the cause of these problems?"

Edgar inhaled slowly. "Gentlemen, Gatekeeper Electrics is thirty years old. I devoted my working life to producing the highest-quality products in the industry. Now, I'm very embarrassed to report that—" he coughed, "that some of our teams have substituted inferior-grade components into the sets and have failed to take proper care with soldering and assembly. This has caused intermittent failures that are frustrating and dangerous."

Merrill had been watching the five federal officials carefully. He knew in advance that Edgar had planned a full confession. His father, Vernon, had recommended they do a limited recall, without notifying the authorities, by blaming the failures on their subcontractors and parts suppliers. But Edgar had made it clear that he would not do that. This had enraged Vernon, who accused his father, Edgar, of "throwing me under the bus for the fictional value of reputation." At the end of that meeting, Edgar had relieved Vernon of his responsibilities and assumed full control of the company, despite being in his late seventies. Fortunately, his health was good, and his mind was clear—but this was not how he expected to be spending his retirement years.

As Merrill watched Inspector Colby and the others, he realized they didn't look surprised at this news. Certainly this was ominous.

"And to what do you attribute these substitutions and assembly failures?" Colby asked.

This was the real moment of truth. Everything that Edgar Kendrick had worked for was about to be lost.

"Gentlemen, I have learned that it was intentional. This was not the fault of our suppliers or our workers, but rather an attempt to increase profits by charging the government full price for military-grade components, while substituting components of lesser grade at a lower cost. Gatekeeper has cheated the government."

Merrill had been expecting candor, but this was remarkable. His grandfather may have just confessed to criminal conspiracy. The various inspectors looked at each other, but before anyone could say anything, Edgar continued.

"As the owner of Gatekeeper, I am responsible. I have not been active in management for the past five years, but the responsibility falls to me. Perhaps I can tell you what I'd like to do to remediate the problem and see if you can help with it."

"Why should we help you? You're the ones who defrauded us," said the representative from the army.

Edgar shook his head. He looked five years older than when he had walked into the room. "I understand that. What you must know is that I'll likely drive the company into bankruptcy executing a full recall of all damaged sets, particularly since I assume that you'll cancel all current and future contracts. In normal circumstances, I would be protected from losing my personal assets because we are a corporation, but I am willing to put up our home in the Hamptons as additional collateral, as well as our townhouse in Manhattan. I'd like to keep as many of my employees working for as long as I can.

"The only thing I need from you is help retrieving as many of the sets as possible, and perhaps permission to send people out to the various points of debarkation to make repairs on the spot, rather than having them all returned to Brooklyn. With the exigencies of war, our competitors simply don't have the capacity to replace all these sets in a timely fashion. Repair is possible with well-trained crews, and we can quickly bring the radios up to standard if given the chance. Fortunately, there was a pattern to the substitution, so we can quickly secure the needed parts to replace the questionable ones." He inhaled slowly to calm himself. "If there are criminal prosecutions with respect to this matter, I only ask that you give us time to correct the problems first so that we can protect the men in the military who depend on us, and then we'll put ourselves forward for justice." With that, Edgar slumped in his chair, fully spent.

"And when you say, 'We will step forward,' who do you mean by *we*?" Inspector Colby asked.

Edgar cast a glance at Merrill, who quickly responded, "All of us who are responsible for running the company. My grandfather is the sole owner, and my father has been the general manager. Our initial investigation suggests that the company treasurer and our purchasing agent may have also received kickbacks to participate. We really haven't had time to sort it all out since we came to you immediately to get a recall as quickly as possible." He paused for a moment. "And you should know that I have been a member of the board of directors, so I will be involved in any proceedings as well."

The inspector from the navy now spoke up. "But it is my understanding that you have been at sea, Captain Kendrick. Were you really in a position to discover these activities and to act on this information?"

"I had anecdotal evidence that there was a problem and called my father from Halifax just before departing on my last voyage. He assured me that it was an isolated incident that would be corrected. Then, one of the ships in a convoy I was protecting failed to receive a warning because the new Gatekeeper radio onboard failed. In other words, I should have acted with more vigor than I did when I first learned of this."

He realized that he had folded his hands in front of him on the table and that he had squeezed them so tightly they were now frozen in that position. He forced himself to pull them apart.

"Well, gentlemen. Can we take action to remediate the problem? Or do you want to bring charges against us immediately?" Edgar asked.

"You showed up here today without your lawyers. Do you think that was wise?"

"Of course it wasn't wise," Edgar said. "But there is an urgency to this matter that does not usually exist. There are Gatekeeper radios out in the battlefields and on ships at sea that are putting men's lives at risk. If our attorneys were here, it would have taken weeks to settle on the format of these talks and to deny responsibility to whatever degree possible before confessing to the mischief. It just isn't worth the price!" Edgar had become reanimated as he said this, and there was a fire in his eyes, as if he was frustrated that the men on the other side of the table were failing to grasp the seriousness of the problem.

"Could you excuse us for a few moments?" the chief inspector said. "We had expected a very different discussion today, and we need to discuss what you have told us."

"Of course," Merrill said. He stood quickly before his grandfather could object, then moved to help him stand. "We'll be waiting outside in the hallway."

CHAPTER EIGHT
A VERY HIGH-PROFILE TARGET

"Turn to port five degrees."

"Port turn, five degrees."

"Very well."

Kendrick subconsciously looked up and to the left while updating his mental map of the convoy. This was the highest-value convoy he had ever been assigned to protect—and the smallest. It consisted of just one troopship moving at maximum speed with four destroyers steaming as fast as they could to keep up. From the German's point of view, the *Warburton* and its group were guarding the grand prize of them all—the incomparable *Queen Mary*, now painted gray and carrying more than 15,000 American soldiers to England to join the growing queue that would make up the Allied Expeditionary Force. Because her color was so indistinct and her speed so incredibly fast, she was known as the *Grey Ghost*. She could speed her way across the waters at more than thirty knots. Although most destroyers were rated for thirty-five to thirty-eight knots, with all boilers fired, only the newest could keep up such a pace for the entire duration of the trip.

On this crossing, the *Queen Mary* was making frequent zigzags, while the destroyers used their speed—superior to the German vessels—to weave an even more intricate pattern around the ship. The *Queen* had made several crossings with no escorts, given that no U-boat in the world could keep up with her pace. In fact, the *Queen Mary* and *Queen Elizabeth* could both match the speed of a German torpedo. But as the world had learned in such a shocking manner in World War I, a German lying in wait *in front* of a steamer could get off a lucky shot and kill even the mighty *Lusitania*. So, when possible, a destroyer escort fanned out in front of the *Queens* to create a shield from any lurking U-boats.

"Care to hear an interesting story?" Kendrick asked Easton.

"Certainly." Easton was hoping for something about the scandal back in America, so he was slightly disappointed when the captain's story took a decidedly different turn.

"The name *Queen Mary* changed the naming convention that the Cunard Line had followed for many years. All their previous ships had names that ended in the letters *ia,* such as *Lusitania, Mauretania, Albania, Andania,* and so forth."

"Hadn't thought of it like that, but that's right, isn't it?"

"Well, when they decided to build the *Queen Mary*, it was to be the grandest, fastest ship of all time. So the president of Cunard went to King George V and said something to the effect of, 'Sir, we'd like permission to name our new ship after the greatest queen in British history.' What he intended was to name the ship *Queen Victoria*. But King George surprised him by replying, 'Why, what an honor! My wife will be thrilled to have such a great ship named after her.' Of course, Cunard couldn't correct the king, and so he named the ship the *Queen Mary*, forever abandoning their naming convention. Now we have the *Queen Mary* and the *Queen Elizabeth*." Kendrick laughed. "Isn't that a great story?"

Easton smiled. "It is a great story. It shows how easily misunderstandings arise. I wonder if the king knew what Cunard intended and took advantage of the awkward wording to honor his wife or if he thought it was really intended to be named after Mary."

"I'm not sure, of course. The British will never raise the subject, and good King George V is long since dead, while his wife, Queen Mary, is now the Queen Mother of George VI."

"There are a lot of Marys in that family. Isn't the present king married to a Mary as well?"

Kendrick nodded. "I have no idea why we care about British royalty, but in this war, they seem to be a real boost to the morale of the British people. Two queens named Mary at the same time—I hadn't thought of that."

"And a third *Queen Mary* that we are panting and wheezing to keep ahead of."

"It is a magnificent ship, isn't it?"

"Yes, sir. And filled with the most valuable cargo in the world."

They were interrupted as an ensign approached from behind. "Excuse me, sir."

Kendrick turned. "Yes, Ensign, what is it?"

"With respect, sir, Chief Engineer Calder wishes to speak to you in the aft engine room if possible."

"Tell the chief I'll join him immediately. You've got the conn, Mr. Easton!"

"First officer has the conn!" Easton said loudly.

Kendrick ducked out the door and made his way through the midwinter gloom to the back of the ship where he could descend into the aft engine room. As soon as he entered, he felt the heat.

"Mr. Calder, it's really hot in here!"

"Yes, sir. That's the problem. We've been running everything at near maximum since leaving New York City, and the engines are showing the strain."

"Are we in danger of losing power?"

Calder sighed. "No, sir. So far everything is working, although I'm worried about one of the shafts on this aft turbine. It is taking an awful lot of lubricant to keep it from binding up. Is there any relief in sight?"

"One more day and we are within range of British aircraft. My understanding is that the British are sending their own destroyers out to meet us. We'll likely break off at that point and do some sweeps of the ocean."

"We'll be out of fuel by then, if you don't mind my saying so."

Kenrick smiled. "Fortunately, a tanker is supposed to meet us. I know we've had oil stored in every nook, cranny, and bunker on the ship."

"Isn't it something grand that a ship of such size can maintain that speed for all this distance? The amount of fuel she uses is astounding."

Kendrick nodded. "To say nothing of the food! 16,000 mouths to feed three times a day, including the crew. It's rather amazing." He paused. "You invited me down here, Chief. Is there anything else I can help with?"

Calder motioned for him to step into a small side room. It wasn't like anyone could hear them above the noise of the machinery, but the men in the engine rooms had become quite adept at reading lips; they had to if they were going to communicate in this cacophony.

Once inside, Calder said, "I know Mr. Easton has been working on it, sir, but two of my men are at each other's throats. I've tried to keep them separate, both by shift and by location, but there have been fistfights and shoving. It's having a bad effect on the crew."

"He did mention something to me. What do you think is the trouble?"

"I think the trouble is that one of the men is married and the other is seeing a married woman. And there are only three people involved!"

It wasn't funny, but Kendrick could not keep himself from laughing. "Mr. Calder, I promise they don't teach us how to anticipate something like this in officer training. What do you recommend?"

"I'm not trying to go around Mr. Easton. I know this isn't your problem to solve. But with all the pressure of protecting that ghost ship out there, I thought you should be aware of the problem. I think it's serious, and one or the other should be brought up for discipline, more than I can give them."

"I understand. Since Mr. Easton has mentioned it to me, I will ask him for an updated report. Perhaps we can come together on an appropriate course of action."

"Yes, sir." Calder was clearly nervous.

"I'm glad you brought me into your confidence, Chief. You have plenty to worry about without this. If this were peacetime, I'd set up a boxing ring on the main deck and let them pound away at each other until they worked it out. But we'll have to come up with something that works in a war zone. Please rest at ease."

"Thank you, sir."

Kendrick excused himself, turned, and walked by as many men as possible to chat with them briefly. Just a minute or two of conversation with the captain could do miracles for morale, particularly on a stressful voyage like this.

* * *

Kendrick planned to return to his cabin to finish some paperwork and maybe even take a catnap, but then his interphone rang. "Kendrick!" he said sharply.

"Yes, sir. First officer here. We have received a coded communication from the fleet. Seems there are U-boats lurking up ahead, and we've been given a course correction."

"I'll be right up!"

Kendrick bounded up the stairs and onto the bridge. Easton handed him the printed message. "Okay then. The *Queen Mary* is heading northeast on her own while we surge ahead on an intercepting path with the wolfpack." Kendrick rubbed his hands. "This is a dicey one. The transport will be heading into ice, which is never a good thing. But she can pour on everything she's got to evade them. Meanwhile, we'll steam ahead and do our best to slow them down and hopefully destroy them. Looks like we're in for a shoot-out." There was no fear in his voice, just excitement. Easton liked that.

Kendrick leaned close to Easton. "John, you still have the conn. Bring us on to the new course and hold steady at thirty-two knots. We really must watch our oil consumption now. It wouldn't do to get there and have nothing left with which to maneuver. I'll pass along the new instructions to the other destroyers." He paused while thinking through the next steps. "I'll order one of the destroyers to parallel the transport so she's not entirely alone out there. Even a ghost needs a friend in such unfriendly waters. The rest of us will make ready for the battle."

"Yes, sir!"

Kendrick noticed the excitement in Easton's voice as well.

* * *

For the past five hours, the crew had been engaged with a U-boat, periodically dropping depth charges, and those not engaged with dropping depth charges watched carefully for torpedo tracks in the water heading their way. As of now, it was still a standoff. Kendrick was feeling frustrated, particularly since this was a voyage like no other he'd been on.

The U-boats had not anticipated the Allies' battle strategy, which was a real advantage. While the British could frequently intercept and decode German orders to their ships at sea, the Germans were less able to do so with British and American signals. It was obvious that the Germans had been waiting for the *Queen Mary* to come into their sights and were frustrated that she was not with the destroyers. This meant they were now unleashing their full fury against the Americans' small armada of tired and fuel-starved destroyers instead.

"It must be a saboteur," Kendrick mused.

"Excuse me, sir? Was that intended for me?"

Kendrick turned to his gunnery officer. "Sorry, Mr. Pendleton. I was just thinking out loud."

"You said something about sabotage, sir?"

Kendrick leaned his head back as far as he could, then raised and lowered his shoulders in a circling motion to relieve the stress. "I was just thinking about how the Germans could anticipate that the *Queen Mary* would be on this track. I am sure they have spies in New York who notified them that she was sailing. But there are a lot of different routes to follow. What are the odds that this wolf pack would choose the exact same course we're on?"

"Not high. You think someone gave away the route?"

"It makes me sick to think so. You know the British have an office for their British Security Coordination somewhere in Manhattan. I guess spying is big business everywhere."

Chief Gunnery Officer Pendleton nodded. "I'm not sure, but I believe I have a brother in the Office of Strategic Services. Maybe he is; maybe he isn't—he won't talk about anything he does. It's all very secretive, and he shows up with souvenirs from the strangest places. But it would be like him to be a spy. I personally like a good honest fight, where you see the enemy and they can see you and you punch it out with each other."

"I suppose I'm like you, as long as our side wins. From what little I know, our spies are doing some tricky things to throw the Germans off their game." Kendrick glanced swiftly over the plot, then motioned for Pendleton to join him. "I need to know what to expect from your torpedo crew if a very specific circumstance arises."

"What are you thinking, sir?"

"I've heard—though I haven't ever seen it—that the Germans have installed snorkels on some of their U-boats so they can fire up their diesels even while submerged. The snorkels also allow them to draw fresh air into the boat. We've held this boat that we've been pursuing down for a long time now. They've fired on us twice, and we've pounded them with depth charges. Their captain must be worried about his batteries. He's either got to slink away and surface, then perhaps attack us head-on, or he may try to use his snorkel if he has one."

Pendleton nodded. "With night falling, he may think he can get away with it."

"Exactly. We'd see a feather in the water if they were moving in the moonlight. But if they are fully stopped, there will be no track."

"So, how can we spot him?"

"You can't hide diesel exhaust. It's not likely that we'll see smoke in the dark, but it would create a smudge against the horizon. I've never been a fan of moonlight, since our profile will stand out like it's illuminated in neon lights. But if we can get our men to look for a shimmering movement in the stars, it would suggest they're venting their diesels."

"Could our radar detect the snorkel?"

"If we're close enough. It's a very small profile, but our operators can orient their search closer in. I just wish something would show up on sonar, so we could know where he's at."

"My guess is he's found a quiet spot and is just waiting." Pendleton was thoughtful. "You started with a question, sir. My guess is that you want to know if I can hit him with a torpedo if we do find him. It's a tough spot, but if your spotters can get me a bearing, I promise I'll figure out the depth."

Kendrick nodded. "Good man. That is exactly what I wanted to know. We'll have to keep ship operations as normal as possible so they don't suspect. I know it is cold out there, but could you go down and speak with your torpedomen directly?"

"Yes, sir. I will also speak with the gunners just in case he surfaces. Our first warning then is likely to be a shell headed our way."

"Thank you."

Kendrick called a brief meeting with his leadership team. They were steaming in a tight circle in search of the U-boat they had been dancing with since early morning, with the constant risk of a counterattack. He had to do something. They'd held this fellow down long enough that he was no longer a threat to the *Queen Mary*.

"The question is, do we hang around a bit longer, hoping this snorkel plan will work, or do we try to catch up with the *Queen Mary* and potentially stir up any other U-boats that may have gotten past our screen?"

"We know our group sank two U-boats for sure," Chief Gunnery Officer Pendleton said. We've been cagey with this fellow, so that's a third. Our best estimate is that there were five boats in the pack, and we know that two of our friends are also holding their own U-boats down. So, potentially, we have them all tied up. But you never know if there was a sixth or seventh, so we're still fairly blind."

"Thank you, Mr. Pendleton. Excellent synopsis." Kendrick paused. "I sent one destroyer to parallel the transport, and we've dispatched a second to run an outer sweep. I think I'll send the *Cargill* on ahead to create yet another buffer."

"Which means we can stay here and still try to get this fellow?" Easton piped up.

Everyone in the group turned at the sound of Easton's voice. For his part, Easton covered a large yawn. He had been taking a forced nap after having been on duty for nearly twenty-four hours since receiving the diversion order.

Kendrick laughed. "Yes, I guess that's what it means."

"All right," Easton said to the group. "My guess is we have no idea where the U-boat is or we'd be depth charging it as we speak."

"So that's what we forgot! To keep track of where the little bounder is," the chief navigator said. As a quartermaster, he was lower in rank than the others, but he had the best sense of humor.

Easton bowed, pretending it was a compliment.

"All right," Kendrick said. "I'm going to stay on point for three more hours. We are very vulnerable. Keep up the search pattern, but I want our radar trained to the surface. They can stay submerged up to three days, but if they want to launch an attack, and I'm sure they do, they'll want to top off their batteries. You all know what we're looking for?" The group nodded. "Then let's find us a U-boat!" Kendrick's last sentence excited the men. They would now pass this information along to the crew to help buoy their spirits.

* * *

Two hours later, after a seemingly endless pattern of circling in ever wider sweeps, a lookout called down to the bridge. "Something odd on the horizon at 120 degrees. A distortion of some kind. Range indeterminable." It would be indeterminable, since judging the horizon at night was notoriously difficult. But the sighting was something.

"All right," Kendrick said quietly to the navigator. "Plot a sweep that brings us to that coordinate, say 2,000 yards out from here. Then give that to the helmsman." He then called down to his chief communications officer and asked him to get ready to concentrate a radar sweep in that direction as soon as they reached the outer edge of their circle. Sonar was not likely to be helpful if the U-boat was just under the surface.

Then Pendleton stepped forward to direct his people.

For the first time, Kendrick noted that his mouth was exceedingly dry. He reached for the now-cold cup of tea and took a few drafts into his parched mouth. As they started their sweep, it would be possible for the U-boat to fire off torpedoes in a spread pattern that would be difficult to evade. He moved over to the helmsman and cupped his hand as he leaned in to speak with him. The helmsman shook his head in acknowledgement. Kendrick then moved to the navigator and repeated the same action.

"Alert the lookouts to watch for torpedo tracks. If that is a U-boat over there with a snorkel up, he can also have his periscope up to get a firing solution on us."

"Aye, sir," Easton said, and he passed the order along. Kendrick had the conn and was directing all the ship's movements.

"Sir, we're one quarter of the way through the turn," the navigator said, startling half the men on the bridge.

"Helm, execute my previous order!"

"Aye, sir, turning toward course 0120."

"Very well! Lee helmsman, order full speed ahead!"

"Aye, sir! Flank speed!"

Men had to grab on to whatever was nearby to avoid being tipped over by the sudden change in course coupled with full acceleration.

"Mr. Pendleton," Kendrick continued, "assume we have a target, and ready your torpedoes. Range to be provided momentarily."

The messenger spoke up, "Sir, lookouts report torpedoes in the water!"

"Course?" Easton spoke into his headset for a few moments. "It looks like they're heading in front of us and will pass to port!"

Kendrick grinned. "Got you!"

Easton shook his head in amazement. How had the captain known to make the unscheduled turn and accelerate?

"Navigator, plot the track of the torpedoes to give me a range."

The messenger tipped his headset to the side as he listened for one of the many messages that came through, and then he spoke up. "Sir, radar reports a contact, course 0120, range 1,000 yards!"

"I confirm that course," the navigator said. It was ironic that modern electronics had to be confirmed by a slide ruler.

"Mr. Pendleton, assume they are diving and moving forward at full battery speed. Then set for that depth and range. Fire torpedoes when ready."

"Aye, sir!" Pendleton hesitated for a moment, then spoke into his interphone. Kendrick registered the sound of compressed air releasing two torpedoes from outside the bridge.

The messenger spoke up. "Sir, lookouts report another torpedo running toward us. Track shows it's dead on to our bow!"

"Hard to starboard, helm! Mr. Pendleton, this new information confirms that they'll be facing us, so do we send another spread?"

Pendleton closed his eyes while picturing the scene in his mind, quickly running through the best options. "Yes, sir."

"Then make it so!"

The ship was groaning as it made an even tighter turn to the right. Out on the deck, men would be falling on the wet metal surface, perhaps cursing as they did so. But this turn should give them enough time to evade this new threat if they could maintain speed.

"Helm, steady as she goes!"

The helmsman ended the turn and started the ship on a forward track. This would make it very tricky for Pendleton.

"Mr. Pendleton, do I need to come back to port?"

"No, sir. We have calculated for an angled shot off the port tubes. Ready when you are, sir."

Kendrick shook his head. "Then fire, Mr. Pendleton. Do fire!"

He heard a second round of whooshing, this time from the left side of the ship.

"Sir, our first spread of torpedoes missed their target," Pendleton said. Bad news.

"Sir, the third German torpedo has passed our port side. A miss by perhaps twenty yards," Easton said. Good news.

"I do *not* want to miss!" Kendrick said this to no one in particular and in such a way that everyone on the bridge knew not to reply. "Time to target?"

"Thirty seconds," Pendleton replied.

Kendrick inhaled slowly and deeply, then held his breath as he stepped outside on the wing of the bridge. It was bracingly cold, but the view forward was unrestricted. He glanced down and saw the gun crews adjusting the angle of their barrels to match the forward progress of the ship. As the countdown reached ten, he started to let his breath out very slowly. "Nine and eight and seven and six and five and—"

Then a brilliant flash of light on the horizon. It took perhaps two seconds for the sound of the concussion to reach them.

Kendrick heard shouts inside the bridge. But they were subsumed by a second flash. Kendrick should have turned away to protect his night vision, but this was a moment to savor. Rather than cheer, he smiled. "Off by five seconds on the first one, just right on the second, Mr. Pendleton," he said to himself. There was a good chance that his counting of the seconds was a bit too slow and that Pendleton got it just right. But either way, their torpedoes had found their mark.

Kendrick stepped back onto the bridge. "All ahead slow!"

"All ahead slow," the lee helmsman said, and in a few moments, Kendrick felt the ship slow in the water.

"Keep a sharp lookout," he heard Easton say. There was always the risk that if they had hit the U-boat in the stern, the Germans could still launch another round of torpedoes against the *Warburton*.

No, they couldn't! Kendrick thought to himself. *If any of them lived, they are deaf and bleeding from the concussion.* It was highly unlikely any of the Germans had survived. Maybe if the bulkhead doors had been closed at the time of the explosion, a few could survive. Otherwise, the blast would have reverberated from one end of the U-boat to the other.

As they came upon the scene, where oil was now burning on the surface, Kendrick asked if there were survivors in the water.

"None seen," came the reply.

Fifty some men dead. Kendrick felt the exhilaration drain from his mind and down into his body. It was a kill. They would wait for a few more minutes just in case someone managed to survive. But then they would have to head for the rendezvous point. He was doubtful they could catch the *Queen Mary*, but even if they didn't, they could still add to the number of Allied eyes watching the ocean to protect her. How long had it been since that long-ago order to turn to port five degrees? That was the moment when all this had started. It felt like a hundred years ago.

"All stop!"

"All stop!"

"Very well."

CHAPTER NINE
REASSIGNED TO ENGLAND

Weymouth, England

"You look flummoxed, Captain."

Kendrick realized he had been biting his lower lip. That always got him into trouble. "No, sir. I'm fine. Of course we'll operate out of Portland—whatever is needed."

"But something is still troubling you."

Kendrick looked up at Admiral Nicholas Luekenga, his commanding officer here in England, who had just informed him that the *Warburton* was to be permanently reassigned to Portland on the southwestern coast of England under Luekenga's command. Kendrick would no longer report to a commanding officer in the United States. Fortunately, he and Admiral Luekenga had a long history of knowing each other, and he respected the admiral's experience and judgment. In fact, Kendrick had been pleasantly surprised to learn that it was Luekenga to whom he was to report here in Weymouth when he received the summons. As to why the *Warburton* was being officially reassigned to the European theater, no reason had been given, but Kendrick suspected his ship was to play a supporting role in the invasion of France—something that the Allies had been working toward for the past two years.

"Something is troubling you . . ." Luekenga prompted a second time. It snapped Kendrick out of his thoughts.

"Yes, sir. I have some troubles not related to the service back home in New York that need attention. I'm just trying to figure out how to work that out. It was workable when the *Warburton* was assigned to Brooklyn. I should communicate with my . . ." He broke off. After all, it was not Luekenga's problem to solve.

"I don't mean to intrude, but you are one of my senior officers. May I ask if this has something to do with your father's situation? I don't know much, but it was in the newspapers." Luekenga waited, but Kendrick held back. "Merrill, it's me, Nick. Talk to me." Kendrick and Luekenga had been friends for more than a decade, most recently working together on the officer leadership training program.

Kendrick exhaled slowly. "Yes, sir. As a result of what happened to my father, my grandfather has been thrust into managing his company after several years in retirement. Part of me feels that I should be there helping him through what is a crisis for our family and his company." He raised his gaze. "But my heart is here, in the battle!"

Luekenga motioned for Kendrick to sit down. "Merrill, I know this is a personal concern. But because Gatekeeper Electrics impacts so many of us in the military, I'd like you to tell me what happened if you are at liberty to do so. Perhaps it is a good idea for you to return and help your grandfather. He certainly deserves support. That is a decision I need to be involved in. I hope you'll tell me about this without embarrassment."

Kendrick was annoyed. He did not want to be discussing this with his field officer, but he realized that Luekenga was well within his rights. "Yes, sir—Nick. The long and the short of it is that my grandfather created Gatekeeper with a primary emphasis on equipment for the military. My father took the company over and, unbeknownst to us, started taking shortcuts and using inferior components to increase profit margins. That has caused equipment failures that puts missions and people at risk. I, myself, was guarding a ship that might have been saved had it not been for the failure of a Gatekeeper radio." He paused to catch his breath. Luekenga kept silent. "At any rate, when I figured out what was happening, I confronted my father and grandfather. My father stormed out—he is a very proud man—and my grandfather reasserted control. I think my father was going to challenge my grandfather's mental capacity so he could retain control. So, we went to the War Department to tell them what had happened before my father could act and to request their help in a recall or rehabilitation of all affected sets. Fortunately, we have a good inventory control system, so we know exactly where the defective sets are located."

"That seems rather risky to me. Were you not putting your grandfather in legal danger since he owns the company?"

"Not just my grandfather, but both of us. I am a member of the board of directors. So, there we were, confessing to substandard work." He hesitated. "My grandfather put everything on the line, telling them that he would forfeit all his assets and that we would all face charges but that the only important thing was to replace or repair all those radio sets. He asked for time to make things right before the 'sword of justice falls,' so to speak."

"So, your father? Did he know about this meeting?"

Kendrick sighed. "That was the shock for us. The short answer is no, he did not know about the meeting. He was so angry that he might have tried to head us off. What we did not know, my grandfather and I, is that while we were meeting with the War Department, they were in the process of arresting my father. They had already learned of the fraud through a tip from a company employee. The officials we were meeting with told us they were planning to come for us next, which is why they were surprised when we requested the meeting."

Luekenga shook his head. "This is like a detective story for me. What happened? Why are you here?" He did not add "instead of in jail," but Kendrick could tell that's what he was asking.

"Well, after we told them about the fraud and offered to turn over all our assets to finance a recall or replacement for every single set, they excused themselves and left us to wonder what was going to happen. It must have been ten minutes, although it felt like an hour."

"And?"

"*And* when they returned, they told us that because of our honesty and because of the quality of Gatekeeper products prior to this lapse, they would place a hold on any criminal charges, and they would offer oversight while we implemented the repairs or replacements. They insisted that my grandfather continue operations, which he had planned to do anyway." Kendrick sat on his hands, out of sight, to steady himself.

"What about the future of the company?"

He looked up. "That was the real miracle. They told us that as long as we'd accept inspectors in the plant, they'd continue to give us new orders, recognizing that to cut off new orders would force the company, and my grandfather, into bankruptcy without resources to execute the recall." He took a moment to breathe. "That was the biggest surprise of all. One minute we fully expected to be arrested, then fifteen minutes later, we learned that the company would survive and we could make good on all the damage. Even now, my grandfather is sending out teams to all the major shipyards to make on-the-spot repairs or to replace defective sets. Production has moved to a twenty-four-hour cycle to make new sets as quickly as possible." He shook his head. "Just kind of unbelievable."

"I assume from the fact that you're here and your grandfather is in charge back home that the War Department feels that he is living up to his commitment."

"Yes. But his position is still on a probationary basis. I think they were prepared to arrest my grandfather that day. Right now, we are operating under their supervision with the understanding that if the repairs are successful, they will defer and eventually stand back from any charges, which makes it crucial that the company act with the utmost integrity from this point forward."

Luekenga shook his head. "And your father?"

"He's out on bail, but he had to surrender his passport. They published the charges against him to discourage other war profiteers. It is a huge embarrassment for the family. My mother won't speak to me, and my grandmother is worried about her husband going back to work under such pressure. I tried calling my father, but he hung up the phone. My guess is that he will be convicted; I'll testify against him if it comes to that." He swallowed. "I hope it doesn't come to that."

"You acted with honor."

"Men were dying . . . and it was our fault."

"I understand." Luekenga stood. "Captain, at this time, please execute the orders I've given you. You are uniquely suited for a mission that is coming up shortly. Once that is done, perhaps you should go back to New York and help your grandfather. I will talk with my superiors about all of this and get back to you."

"But, sir—"

"There are many ways to fight a war, Merrill, and having reliable equipment is one of them. But for now, we cannot spare you, so please keep your ship at the ready. I can't tell you anything more than that right now, but what we have in mind is vital."

"Thank you, sir." That was all he could say. Kendrick was simultaneously thrilled and miserable.

* * *

Brooklyn, New York

"What do you think, Joe?" Edgar Kendrick asked.

Joe shook his head. This was the greatest opportunity of his life, and yet he felt it was completely unrealistic to even contemplate.

"I'm flattered," he said to Edgar. "But . . ." He lifted his left hand. While he had regained some use of his hand, it was still difficult to control, and it tired quickly whenever he tried to work on a radio set. "I mean, I'd love a job, but I don't think I could keep up with the pace, at least not yet." He had stayed at Merrill Kendrick's apartment in Manhattan after the fireworks at Edgar's home a month earlier. He wanted to go back home to Boston, but Merrill had insisted he stay, promising that he would have a job at Gatekeeper Electrics if they could keep the company together. With everything that Merrill's grandfather had been through, he was only now talking with Joe about employment. But now that it was a real offer, Joe was embarrassed by his disability and felt that he really should go back to Boston.

"Joe, I should have been more specific. I don't want to hire you to work on the assembly line. I want to hire you to lead a new department I'm creating to assure quality control in all our departments. It will be the responsibility of individual operating departments to keep standards high, but this new group will create protocols to assure that we adhere to strict purchasing guidelines, component controls, and scheduled and unscheduled inspections of both the assembly lines and the finished products before they ship. Your group can shut down an assembly line anytime a problem is discovered, with no one able to override your decision."

Joe's eyes widened. The idea itself was terrific. As far as he knew, no one in the industry had a "quality control" department. But to put a Japanese man in charge? "Thank you, Mr. Kendrick. I think it's great idea, but not with me in charge."

"But you are the perfect person for it. We have great men and women at the factory, but they have all been part of the corrupted culture. I need someone from the outside who can look at our systems and processes with a clear, unbiased eye. What I want most is someone who knows how to build a set, tear it down, reassemble it, and make it work in battle conditions. And I don't have anyone with that skill set, except you."

"That makes sense." But Joe glanced down at his arm and leg. "But I have two strikes against me. I don't know a single Japanese person who is in a leadership role, except in non-command roles in all-Japanese units in the army. Even there, their senior officers are white. And second, why would anyone take orders from someone who is crippled? It just doesn't make sense. Maybe I could be on the team—"

Edgar Kendrick was an idealist—and remarkably without prejudice. "Joe, people wouldn't hold it against you that you were injured in war. They'll respect that."

"Are you sure about that, sir? I've heard rumors that President Roosevelt has some kind of disability, but they hide it from the public. If even he is afraid to show a physical limitation, what chance would I have?"

Edgar nodded slowly. "That is true. The Roosevelts were our neighbors in Manhattan. He had polio that left his legs pretty much useless. You'll notice that he always has someone walk with him, to hold him up. He even has one of his sons stand by his side when he gives a speech."

"And he isn't Asian-American. I honestly doubt that we could find people to work on a team that I'm in charge of. And I cannot begin to imagine what will happen if I shut down an assembly line that was being led by a white man. I'm not sure you understand how deeply ingrained—" He stopped. There was no reason to say more.

"I've thought of that, Joe. I understand it is a real problem. But you should know a few things. First, almost eighty percent of our assembly line people are from ethnic minorities, and almost half of them are women. They are hard workers and very dedicated. I honestly don't think they'd have a problem with you as a leader."

"And the other twenty percent?"

"The other twenty percent are going to be too busy doing their jobs to worry about you doing your job." Edgar sometimes had the appearance of a kindly old gentleman, but in this moment, Joe saw the steel in his personality that had enabled him to build a large and successful company. "These people report to me. I will not tolerate insolence on their part or discrimination. We are under too much pressure for that."

He waited, but Joe said nothing. "Joe, everyone on your team will be volunteers. They will know in advance who they will be reporting to. So you should not have problems on that count. I plan to make it clear to everyone in the factory that the quality control unit is a personal extension of me and that any insult to you is an insult to me. The other twenty percent are my leaders. They will agree in advance, or they will be replaced. I'm really very committed to this."

Joe smiled. "Mr. Kendrick, I wish everyone was like you. But for your sake, as well as mine, I'd like you to talk with your managers first. I think you also need to talk to the War Department about the inspectors they are going to insert into the factory—I'm not sure they'd accept your idea. If all those parties say they will try it, I'll consider it. But if they resist, then it is better for everyone if we choose a different battle. My parents' homeland is at war with the United States, and most people in America think it's a problem to have someone like me anywhere near a war production plant. Besides, I've got plenty on my plate already."

"All right. But I think you'll be surprised. Men should be judged on their abilities, nothing else. In the meantime, I want to start you on the payroll to look through our schematics and to assess the easiest way for us to make repairs. No one reporting to you—just your assessment of how we can fix things."

Joe nodded. *I'm sure one of us will be surprised,* he thought to himself. "That sounds good. I promise to give you my best effort."

CHAPTER TEN
CHASING E-BOATS
IN THE ENGLISH CHANNEL

"Tell me again why the Germans do all their raiding at night." Easton yawned.

"Because our air cover would blast them to smithereens if they came out in the daylight," replied Chief Gunnery Officer Pendleton. "The so-called 'invincible' Luftwaffe has all but been destroyed here in France, and it's doing little better in Russia. Hermann Göring has managed to misuse his air force in whatever theater it operates."

"Ah," Easton said. He hadn't really expected an answer to his question; it was more his way of complaining to himself that he was tired of being out in the English Channel at 0200 searching for German E-boats. But now he decided he had a real question. "So, tell me again the difference between a German E-boat and an S-boat?"

"There is no difference. It's just the German version of a torpedo boat. The Germans call it an S-boat for *Schnellboot*, meaning a fast boat. The British decided to call it an E-boat for *enemy boat*. Just like how the British call the country Germany instead of Deutschland. Why can't people call a country by the name that the people who live there call it?"

Now it was Easton's turn to have an answer. "*Germany* is from the Roman name for *Deutschland*: 'Germania.' Almost all the Roman provinces ended in *ia* like Britannia, Hibernia, Caledonia, Italia . . ."

Pendleton laughed. "And how on earth do you know all that? Hibernia? Where the blazes is Hibernia?"

"Ireland. Caledonia is Scotland; Italia is Italy; and Hispania is Spain. I guess England is choosy in which places they keep the Roman names for. But to the Germans it is Deutschland, their historic name for the place."

"Okay, Mr. Easton, since you brought all this up, what's the difference between Britain and England?"

"Great Britain, using the shortened version of the Roman name Britannia, is the former countries of England, Scotland, and Wales, now united. 'Eng-land' is the short version of 'Angle-land' for the Anglo-Saxons who settled there. It's confusing to us outsiders."

Pendleton smiled. It was often tedious at sea, and he loved that in Easton he had a kindred spirit who could find such pleasure in historical details like this.

An ensign approached, drawing Easton's attention. "Sir, lookout reports a blinking light bearing 095."

"Thank you." With that, Easton and Pendleton's colloquy about name trivia ended abruptly as they moved quickly to their respective battle stations.

Challenging an E-boat was a dicey business since it had a top speed of forty-three knots compared to the *Warburton*'s thirty-eight. Plus, the E-boats were nimbler, with a miniscule 100–ton displacement versus 2,900 tons for the destroyer. Given the right conditions, the German torpedo boats could maneuver into an ideal torpedo shot using their smaller profile to make quick course changes. But on the other side of the ledger, the *Warburton* had its five-inch guns, which could fire on the torpedo boats from a relatively safe distance. Early detection and setup for battle were the keys to success.

"I don't see anything," Easton said. "Get a precise fix from the lookout who spotted it."

The command was repeated to the lookout, who confirmed his first report.

"What I'd give for even the slightest hint of a moon." The sky overhead was filled with clouds, right on the edge of stormy. "Or to have the winds come up." The E-boats often retreated to the safety of their anchorage if the waves became too choppy for such a small craft.

"There—I believe I see movement at the area indicated," Pendleton said, motioning to Easton. "If he was using his signal lamp, that means there are more than one of them out there. And with the small convoy making its way out to the Atlantic, there are a lot of targets."

"Time to let them know we're here." Easton turned to the communications officer and gave the order for radar to sweep the horizon in the indicated area. One of the paradoxes of radar was that while it made the enemy visible to the *Warburton*, it was also detectable by the Germans. Once alerted to the presence of Allied warships, the E-boats would often turn tail and race back to the French shore—and safety. But with the convoy out tonight, that would be okay—Easton would be happy if the Germans returned to shore without ever firing on the convoy. A battle avoided was as good as a battle won, in this case. "Notify the captain that we are going to battle stations."

"Aye, sir. Notify the captain!"

Kendrick was on the bridge almost before the corpsman could confirm that he had been notified. "Report, Mr. Easton!"

Easton motioned to the plot. "Radar lit up like a Christmas tree, sir. It looks like there are four E-boats out there. They are taking evasive action right now, but it doesn't look like they're turning for home."

"My guess is that they have intelligence that this convoy is coming through. This convoy includes two troopships that are making a beeline for open water to support actions in the Mediterranean, so this situation is high stakes."

"I suspected as much," Easton said. "It probably saves nearly a week of travel time not having to go north up and around Scotland, but it also puts the troopships in harm's way here in the channel."

"Which is why we're here." Kendrick walked over to Pendleton. "Are any of those boats within range of our guns?"

"Just barely out of range, I'm afraid. They have enough speed that they can keep their distance. We could outwit them if we didn't have to use radar."

"Too dangerous. Better to know where your enemy is than to guess." Kendrick approached the navigator. "How long before the convoy is supposed to arrive at this point?"

"Approximately twenty minutes, sir."

Easton tipped his head back and closed his eyes. "We have three destroyers running a screen for the troopships, and we make a fourth playing the role of sweeper."

In soccer, *sweeper* would describe a defensive player with no pre-assigned position. The sweeper's job was to intercept the ball wherever it was on the field, and that was exactly what the *Warburton* was supposed to do in this battle. Kendrick liked the assignment, since it provided him freedom, but it was also the role with the greatest responsibility.

Kendrick turned to the navigator. "Any news on any British motor torpedo boats?"

"Yes, sir. There are four moving as an additional screen for the transports."

Kendrick shook his head, then turned to Easton. "Who wouldn't want to bet on the team with four destroyers and four motor torpedo boats against four German E-boats?"

"And yet you're not smiling."

"No, I'm not. It's because both the British MTBs and the German E-boats are so maneuverable. There's a lot of water out here, and all they have to do is slip between us with enough time to fire off a spread of torpedoes and *wham*—several thousand men are killed." He paused. "And we're not at all sure there aren't more than four of the E-boats. These are just the ones in our neighborhood."

Easton spoke up. "Sir, I just picked up what I believe is the lead ship in the convoy. It's most likely a destroyer ahead of the van."

"Very well." Kendrick turned to the radio operator. "Send a message to all ships in the area that reads: 'German E-boats present—four confirmed, total not yet known. Implement zigzag pattern, and small warships, move to intercept.'"

"Yes, sir. Make message to the fleet . . ." The radio operator confirmed the balance of message, sent it, and then confirmed it was sent. One by one, the other warships started responding to the broadcast.

"What's our status on catching up to the E-boats?" Kendrick asked the navigator.

"They've started moving out from shore, and we are closing the distance, sir."

"Mr. Pendleton, prepare to fire some star shells approximately five minutes from now when the scene tightens up."

"Yes, sir. Star shells." Pendleton passed the order up to the fire-control center located above and behind the bridge.

"Lee helmsman, flank speed. I want to close the distance so our star shells can do their job."

"Flank speed—aye, aye, sir!"

Kendrick found that he relished the sound of the repeater, in which the change in speed was indicated on the bridge, then confirmed by the engine room. Turning to Easton, he added, "One thing about operating in the channel is that we don't have to worry about fuel. I can go to flank speed without fretting that we might run out a couple hundred miles short of our port."

"Yes, sir." Easton smiled. He had been in battle with Kendrick often enough now that he realized the captain always made some kind of positive statement just as they were about to engage the enemy. He assumed it was Kendrick's way of girding himself up for the battle.

"There it is!"

Easton also knew what Kendrick meant by this. It was the change in the vibration under their feet as the ship worked its way up to maximum speed. With the ocean rather choppy that night, it made for a bucking sensation as they bounded over the waves.

"Sir, we are in range for star shells."

"Thank you, Mr. Pendleton. Fire at your discretion."

"Aye, sir!"

At this point, Kendrick stepped out onto the open wing. There was nothing in battle that he enjoyed more than the star shells. He listened as the aft guns concussed and then followed the trajectory of the shells in a great arc as they moved up into the sky. As soon as they ignited into a slow-burning magnesium fire, a parachute held them in the air for as long as possible to provide illumination to the scene.

Thus was the darkness dispelled, and he saw the sleek profile of the German E-boats as they headed on a steepening angle to the coast, trying to travel west of the lead destroyer in the convoy while moving out farther into the channel. Their task was to find an opening between the screening ships and the transports to fire off their torpedoes. When the last star lit up, he also noticed the British motor torpedo boats off to the portside making their move toward the German E-boats. Meanwhile, the destroyers had moved closer to their charges in the convoy. While he had observed all of this on the radar screen, it was easier to visualize out here in the cold spring air with his own eyes.

He spoke into his headset. "Mr. Pendleton, can you fire on any of those E-boats?"

"Yes, sir. Although the way they're maneuvering will make it difficult to land a blow."

"Go ahead and fire anyway. I want to give them lots to think about as they try to kill our boys. If they have to worry about MTBs, destroyers, *and* five-pound shells, they'll have a harder time doing their dirty work. Set up a pattern that is likely to catch them in their turns. Please fire at your discretion."

"Yes, sir." Pendleton gave directions to the fire-control center, who transmitted the firing solutions to the five-inch gun crews. These men were remarkable—manually loading and firing up to twenty shots per minute.

Kendrick found it odd being in a battle inside the close quarters of the channel. He found that he liked dealing with surface ships, rather than U-boats, since you could keep your bearings without hours of guessing, searching, and worrying about a submerged target. Here, the battle was open and two dimensional—much easier to keep track of. *Except for torpedoes. Once you see a torpedo running, there's not a lot of time to react.*

"Sir, it looks like the odds have shifted. Radar has picked up four more E-boats moving out from a cove."

"Very well."

Kendrick moved back inside and went immediately to the plotting table. The new German boats were moving toward the rear of the convoy. With the convoy heading west and the *Warburton* steaming east at flank speed, they were the ones best suited to engage this new threat.

"Come to course 085," Kendrick ordered. This put them on a new track that allowed him to position the *Warburton* between this new threat and the last transport in the line. The E-boats were faster, but the *Warburton* had a head start.

"Mr. Pendleton, there are too many for us to handle with torpedoes. Your gunners have got to break up this new formation, hopefully even hitting one or two."

"Yes, sir. If you could steepen the angle of our path, it would make it easier for me to bring our rear guns to bear off the starboard side."

Kendrick complied. "Come to course 078!" Repeated, executed, and confirmed.

"Thank you, sir." Pendleton gave orders.

They were now just a moment away from when the guns could fire. Kendrick noted that the transport that was being pursued executed an evasive action, which gave the *Warburton* a few more minutes. *Anytime, Don, anytime!* Then he saw the flash of the forward guns, followed by the concussion. His mind registered that the rear battery had also opened fire. Now the battle was fully engaged.

"Sir, one of the E-boats has turned on us! Bearing off the starboard side."

"Very well." Of course, it was *not* well; this brave little boat was going to take on the *Warburton* so the other three could attack the transport. "Hold course!" He felt the electricity in the room increase dramatically. "Mr. Pendleton, use your side launcher to send some torpedoes their way—force them to break off the attack."

"Aye, sir. Launching torpedoes off the starboard!" Pendleton's voice tended to increase in both pitch and volume when in battle, and it now reverberated in the bridge, despite the firing of the guns.

"Got one!" This was Easton, who motioned to the horizon.

Kendrick had missed one of the most spectacular sights in battle—a German Schnellboot being hit right in the midships by one of Pendleton's guns. But even having missed the moment of the explosion, he could see its effect: flames on the water and secondary blasts as the ammunition on board the small craft started exploding. It was thrilling. And yet, Kendrick could not forget that men were dying in the flames.

"One down!" Pendleton said. "What about our attacker?"

"Lookouts report that he's spotted our torpedoes," Easton replied. "He's turning . . ." Kendrick hung on to Easton's words next words: "Torpedo running directly toward us!"

"Hard to port!" Kendrick shouted.

"Hard to port!" came the helmsman's reply.

Kendrick counted to ten, then used his glasses to try to spot the torpedo track. "Report!" He waited anxiously as the lookouts, who had the benefit of higher elevation, were also trying to see a track in the darkness.

"Torpedo passing to starboard!" Easton said.

Kendrick acknowledged receiving the report.

"Come back to original bearing!" said Kendrick.

"Aye, sir. Back to seventy-eight degrees," the helmsman confirmed.

The boat that had originally attacked them had completed a quick sweep away from the *Warburton*'s torpedoes and was now swinging around for another attack.

"He's on a fairly predictable path, Mr. Pendleton!"

"Aye, sir!" Both men understood that Pendleton was to use this predictability to use his guns. "All guns coming to bear!" With more than 1,000 rounds of ammunition, the *Warburton* easily outgunned the German boat, and now was the time to use that advantage.

He watched in fascination as the German boat started a new line of attack and then as Pendleton's gunners started bracketing the little ship. The Germans realized the danger too late, having considered only the torpedoes in the *Warburton*'s arsenal. As the splashes and explosions drew close, the boat made an incredibly swift turn to the south, but in doing so, it managed to bring itself directly in line with the last salvo fired from the most forward gun. In a spectacular explosion that lit up the night sky, its slender superstructure lifted up and into the air in what looked like a million shattered pieces.

"Got him!" Pendleton shouted. Then, realizing his outburst, he spoke more calmly. "Excuse me. Got him, sir!"

Kendrick laughed. "Good work, Mr. Pendleton. Two down!"

Then something happened that Kendrick sensed more than thought. It was triggered by motion at the extreme edge of his vision. "The transport—what is it doing?" he asked urgently.

"It's turning toward us, sir," replied the navigator, clearly astonished.

"What on earth!" Easton exclaimed. "He's shortening the distance to the E-boats."

Kendrick shook his head. "He's following the preplanned zigzag pattern. He hasn't reacted to the dynamics of the battle." Kendrick said this loud enough so that everyone could hear and adjust their thinking to this new reality. *The fool!* "Come to port five degrees."

"Sir?" Easton asked quizzically. This maneuver would expose the full flank of the *Warburton* to both E-boats. If ever there was a suicide maneuver, this was it.

"We've got to come between the transport and the Germans." Kendrick inhaled deeply. "Tell the lookouts to tell us the instant they see torpedoes in the water."

His order was relayed.

"Radio the transport and order him to turn to starboard at full speed. Tell him to do it now!"

"Aye, sir. Radio the transport and order turn to starboard at full speed!"

"Very well." Then Kendrick added, "Confirm the order by signal lamp!" He didn't want the captain of the transport to miss the message.

He motioned for Pendleton and Easton to come together at the plot table. "We've got no time. Here's what's got to happen. Don, I need you to launch torpedoes toward those E-boats in as wide a spread as possible. Make them veer off. Concentrate all gunfire to break up their course. Of course, they'll be launching torpedoes any second now. I'll do my best to avoid them, but if it comes to it, we'll take a torpedo hit rather than let it go through to the transport. John, I want you to stand right next to the helmsman so that we can maneuver as tightly as possible. He's really good, but you are better, so guide him or take the wheel yourself."

"Aye, sir."

"Let's get to it."

Pendleton performed superbly. He brought his torpedo launcher to bear and had the torpedoes off in less time than it took most men to think about it. They were too far from the German boats to make an effective shot, but that wasn't the point. It was to have torpedoes running in such a broad pattern that the E-boats had to make as wide a turn as possible to avoid being hit. All Kendrick could hope was that the Germans cared less about killing the transport ship than they did about saving their own lives.

"Our torpedoes are away. Guns bearing now!"

"Very well."

"Sir, torpedo tracks. The E-boats have launched their pattern and are turning away."

"Very well."

He wished desperately that radar could track torpedoes so that he knew where each of them were just now. It was likely that at least four were running, with as many as eight possible.

"Radio transport and tell him to watch smartly so he doesn't crash into us. Advise that we are running interference on torpedoes and stay out of our way!"

"Aye, sir. Radio transport . . ."

Kendrick registered that the rest of the order was confirmed. His stomach hurt, which he noticed for the first time, and realized that it was because he was holding his muscles so tense that it was hard to remember to breathe.

"Sir, I have a quick plot on the path of the five torpedoes we've spotted."

Kendrick moved immediately to the plot table where the navigator showed him the path of each of them. Without moving, he ordered a further turn to port. With the transport finally having made appropriate turns, the *Warburton*'s latest maneuver meant that two of the five torpedoes would pass harmlessly off the stern of the *Warburton* and the transport.

"What about these three? Order the transport to turn hard to port!"

Such a move risked a collision with the *Warburton*, but it took two of the remaining three out of their path. But there was still one that the slower-moving transport simply could not avoid. So, Kendrick gave an order that would place the *Warburton* directly in the path of intercepting the final torpedo. He moved to the interphone and switched on the all-ship intercom.

"Now hear this. Now hear this! This is the captain. Brace for impact of a torpedo headed our way. Clear all forward compartments and seal bulkheads. We've got sixty seconds, so move to protect yourselves!"

He gave one final course correction that was the equivalent of splitting a hair. Once again, he saw Easton look at him quizzically, but he decided not to explain himself. Now it was a matter of seconds. The *Warburton* and the German torpedo were on a collision course, and barring a miracle like a misfire, they were going to be hurt.

"Ten seconds, sir!"

Kendrick resisted the temptation to count down. At just the last moment, he grabbed hold of a railing and looked down. He did not want to be blinded by the flash. Then, just as expected, Kendrick felt the impact before he heard the explosion. The ship shuddered as it lost forward speed from a hit on the starboard side, almost at the bow.

"Reduce speed to all-ahead slow!" Kendrick shouted.

"Reduce speed to all-ahead slow!" confirmed the lee helmsman. Kendrick felt the ship lose speed immediately.

Had he given that order twenty seconds earlier, the *Warburton* would have been spared, but the transport ship would have been struck. He finally looked up and saw a fire burning on the bow of the *Warburton*. "Damage report as soon as you can, John."

Easton was huddled over his small desk, writing furiously as each of the departments reported in.

"What about our other E-boat?" Kendrick asked Pendleton.

"One of our British friends has taken after him. It looks like it's a race to the finish. My guess is they handled the first four and saw our predicament."

With no damage report to tell him what he should do next, Kendrick stepped onto the wing and peered into the darkness. He could see brief flashes on the horizon, which was likely exhaust flames from the British motor torpedo boat. The British used gasoline-powered engines while the Germans used diesel. In a high-speed chase, the British were known to inject kerosene into their fuel line to give an additional burst of power. It wasn't good for the engines and it often gave away their position since flames came out the exhaust ports. But that didn't matter now.

"I hope they get him!" Kendrick said bitterly. He worried about how many of his men on the *Warburton* had been killed or wounded because of that German E-boat.

"Damage-control reports, sir!"

Kendrick quickly returned to the bridge to hear the report.

"Damage is light, sir. We have a hole in the starboard plating at extreme forward, but the bulkhead doors are holding. The chief is reinforcing them now. We should be able to make our own way back to port."

"Injuries?"

"Two men killed in the forward gun. Perhaps six or seven injured down below. The surgeon hasn't made his final report."

Kendrick shook his head. Then he forced himself to relax the muscles in his stomach. "Thank you. Could have been worse, but this is bad enough!"

"Sir, message from the transport."

"Read it."

"Thank you, *Warburton*. You saved us. Regret you were hit."

Kendrick stood stock still. How to reply? It was the transport captain's fault this had happened. Finally, knowing the young signalman would be anxious, he responded. "Acknowledge. Say, 'Glad you are safe. Stay sharp, and safe journey.'"

"Aye, sir." He repeated the message and then left to send it.

"It was that last maneuver, wasn't it, sir?"

Kendrick turned at Easton's voice, confused at the question. "Last maneuver?"

"Yes, sir. That last course change you ordered made it so that the torpedo mostly glanced off us, rather than hitting us straight on. You minimized the damage with that one."

Kendrick nodded. "It was risky. If we had turned too sharply, the torpedo would have gone past us and hit the transport. It really is a game of inches."

"Well, from my point of view, it was amazing."

"Thank you, John. Will you give the orders to get us underway as soon as possible? I'm going to radio the commodore and tell him we don't have the speed to keep up, so the convoy is now someone else's responsibility. Then I'm going down to my cabin. Please keep me alert to any dangers." He paused for a moment. "If we were hit forward, that means one of our largest crew quarters is now out of service."

"Aye, sir. Approximately forty hammocks fully submerged. We'll make arrangements for hot bunking the affected crew." Hot bunking would allow the displaced crew to share beds with others who were awake and on station.

"I'm sure that will make everyone happy." Kendrick was not often sarcastic, but he knew very well that the crew hated hot bunking. "Very good, though. Best of a bad situation."

After he was gone, Easton stepped onto the wing. "He just saved more than 2,000 men using maneuvers that no one has ever thought of, and he's down there sick with himself because of the two who were killed." He shook his head. "Are you sure you want to be in command of your own ship, John?"

CHAPTER ELEVEN
CHANGING ROLES

THE GOVERNMENT INSPECTORS ASSIGNED TO Gatekeeper were unanimous in rejecting Joe Horiuchi as leader of the quality team. This came as an unpleasant surprise to Edgar Kendrick. The response was more subdued from the Gatekeeper managers because they did, after all, report to Edgar. But their lackluster response let him know that they did not like the idea either. So, reluctantly, he had to come up with a new plan.

"Joe, I need to talk with you." The look on Kendrick's face told Joe what was about to happen.

"Yes, sir."

"Joe, your work has been excellent in scoping out our vulnerabilities, and I think we've corrected the problems for all new sets currently in production."

Joe knew this, but he also knew that Kendrick needed to stall for time until he was ready to broach the topic they really needed to discuss. "Yes, sir, I'm pleased with the new sets coming out. I've found just a handful of problems, and none of those were related to the earlier . . . ," he wanted to say *fraud* but thought better of it, ". . . to the earlier production problems."

"What kind of new problems have you found?"

Joe took a deep breath. His boss was clearly on edge. "Nothing to worry about. Just the kind of ordinary errors that show up in any high-speed production line, like an occasional cold solder, a vacuum tube that fails early in its life cycle, or a cracked dial from jostling on the line. They all would have been caught farther down the line if I hadn't pulled them randomly. So, from my point of view, the new production is right up to industry standards."

Edgar nodded. "Okay." That was the most he could come up with.

"Listen, Joe, about our reorganization. I'm afraid that we'll have to do it differently than I hoped."

"Yes, sir. That's not a surprise." Joe immediately wished he hadn't said it like that, since it was the equivalent of saying, "I told you so."

"Yes, well, it is what it is. The government inspectors just felt . . ." Edgar's voice trailed off. He did not need to explain to Joe that the idea of a Japanese man in charge of a crucial department at an essential war industry plant was simply unacceptable while the war with Japan continued—even though Joe had proved his loyalty to the United States more than once, sacrificing his leg and arm in the process.

Edgar continued. "Here's what I've come up with. Daryl Rogier currently supervises final assembly. He has agreed to assume the additional responsibility of managing the quality control team. Daryl thinks highly of you and intends to let you define processes and quality standards, which is exactly what I wanted you to do before. But if we must ever shut down the line or make changes to process, you'll take it to Daryl, and then he'll make the final decision and announce it to the other managers and the government inspectors. You'll be the one making the recommendations but . . ." He hesitated.

"But he'll be the one to enforce them." Joe felt bad that Edgar looked so miserable. "Listen, Mr. Kendrick, I'm fine with this. I prefer it since I don't like confrontations anyway. This will work better. And I don't even mind if he decides to override me. I think of myself as an engineer, not a leader, so I'm fine with this."

Edgar nodded. "Good. I'm glad you see it this way." He wanted to say more, but it would serve no purpose. "We'll have a meeting tomorrow morning to assemble the final team. Then you can get to work on finding faster ways to repair or replace sets out in the field. I may even have you go back to England since a lot of the ships that use our equipment are on station there. You'll go as part of a team that Daryl assigns."

Joe nodded. "A very good plan." He left it at that.

"Well then." Edgar hesitated. "I'm off to meet with some of our government overseers. I need their sign-off on this arrangement, so I'd better get to it."

Joe nodded, and Edgar moved off awkwardly. Joe thought he looked exhausted. *This job will probably kill him.* Joe looked back down at the radio he had been working on. He decided that he really wasn't disappointed at this outcome. It was far better to let Daryl Rogier be the bad guy when things went wrong than him. But he wasn't happy about it either. *Why shouldn't an American, regardless of his descent, be allowed into a leadership role if he is the most qualified?* He was aware of the success being reported by the "Purple Heart Battalion" infantry group in Europe—an all-Japanese fighting unit that was having spectacular success in fighting the Germans. But he was also aware that several senior white officers had tried to falsely discredit the group to get them decertified.

"Maybe someday." He grabbed a soft rag to use in pulling a tube from the radio. "Maybe someday."

CHAPTER TWELVE
OPERATION NEPTUNE

June 1944

"RECALL ALL MEN FROM LEAVE and confine everyone to the ship," Kendrick said. "We need to be ready to steam within twelve hours."

"Aye, sir." Easton did his best to keep his voice steady. For the past four weeks, he had been working long days outfitting the ship while repairs were made in the Portland dockyard. The *Warburton* had limped its way back to port with just one incident—a couple of German fighter aircraft had found them alone in the ocean. The fighters had strafed the ship while Pendleton's gun crews retaliated with anti-aircraft flak. One man on the *Warburton* was wounded by a ricocheting bullet but had recovered. Meanwhile, neither of the German aircraft had been damaged. It was always tough for ground-based guns to hit a fighter in the air—but the effort was still worth it if the blanket of anti-aircraft flak forced the fighters to deviate from their ideal firing path.

After the Germans withdrew, the crew was left with the fear that the Germans would send in some dive bombers, but apparently, there was not enough left of the Luftwaffe to take advantage of such an easy target. Once back in port, the *Warburton* was given priority on repairs, and Easton's hopes of some rest and relaxation in London had turned to ash.

"You were in that meeting for quite a long time," Easton said as easily as possible. He thought it might be worth the trouble to dangle some bait. Everyone in the whole of southwest England was curious about the expected invasion of Europe. The weather had been contrary these first few days of June 1944, but something had to happen soon, or people's heads would explode from anticipation, or at least, that's how it felt to Easton. After all, there was upwards of one and a half million Americans in England waiting for the invasion of the mainland, in addition to all the English, Canadians, and Australians. Something had to happen soon. Easton hoped Kendrick knew something and would tell him.

"Nothing much to report. As you know, Admiral Luekenga is very thorough, and his briefings are . . . also thorough." It was a better word than *long-winded*.

"So, no insights into any major action?"

Kendrick smiled. "John, I've occasionally wondered how I'd hold up to an interrogation by the Gestapo. Would torture break me? Would a threat to my family back in New York be my Achilles' heel? What would get me to talk?" He took a moment to look around. "Of course, I hope that I'd never give anything away, no matter how horrible the treatment, but it's hard to know until you are in the situation."

Easton looked at him with narrowed eyes, knowing full well what was coming.

"I honestly don't know. But," he turned to Easton and smiled, "one thing I know for sure is that I'll never give anything away here in England, even to a friend, and even if I did know something." He pulled his hat a little tighter in a vain attempt to keep the rain off his glasses.

Easton sighed. "It was worth a try."

"Yes, it was. I'm glad that you are too decent a man to use torture, John."

Easton sighed. "By the way, I saw that Japanese friend of yours the other day."

"Joe Horiuchi?"

Easton nodded. "He was with a small group of Americans working in a bunker near the wharves. I talked with him for a few minutes."

Kendrick furrowed his brow. "You do realize that he *is* an American, don't you?" Then, before Easton could respond, he went on. "How is he doing physically?"

"I think pretty well. He walks with a limp but wasn't using crutches. And he told me that he has learned how to manipulate his left arm in such a way that he can do about eighty percent of what he used to do with both hands fully functional. I think he's learned how to improve how he uses his good hand in such a way that he can do everything essential." Easton paused. "Even at eighty percent, he can do ten times more with that electronic equipment than I could ever do, even with both arms."

Kendrick smiled. "Me too. I'm glad he's feeling better. I assume he's over here to replace Gatekeeper sets."

"Or repair them, he said. It turns out that he was able to isolate where all the faulty components were, so they can simply replace those pieces and have the sets at full strength. I think what he's mostly doing here is training the onboard communications specialists how to do the repairs and then giving them the parts they need to get things working right."

Kendrick nodded. "That is good news. I wish I would have seen him. But too late now."

While Kendrick paused, Easton decided to broach a subject that had paradoxically pleased and bothered him. "Sir, if I might ask you a question?"

"Of course. What is it, John?"

Easton cleared his throat, betraying his nervousness. "It's just that I read your most recent write-up about my performance."

"A very positive write-up. Is something bothering you?

"It's just that . . . it's just that . . . ," He straightened. "It's just that you recommended me for promotion, which I appreciate, but—" He hesitated.

"But what? You are qualified for command. I have every confidence in your abilities and your leadership."

"Yes, sir. Thank you. It's just that I have a question about leadership. I hope in explaining myself that I don't offend you, because you are the finest leader I've ever worked with." Easton's face was slightly flushed at this point.

Kendrick motioned for Easton to step closer. "John, there is nothing you can say that will offend me. So just say what's on your mind."

"Yes, sir. It's just that you are extremely reserved in your nature. You are relentlessly encouraging to the crew, and you often express appreciation. But it seems like nothing ever rattles you. You keep your voice flat and unemotional. It is so hard for me to be like that. I'm not sure I could pull it off."

Kendrick nodded. He understood exactly what Easton was getting at. *You are wondering if a captain has to be a person with no friends and no emotions—at least, no expressed emotions. That is who I've become, and outside this ship, where has it got me? A social recluse?* He shook his head.

"Here's what I can tell you, John. All but one of the captains I served under felt it was their job to remain steady and calm no matter what the circumstances. But it took a toll; I once passed by the closed door of one of my captains and heard him unleash a tirade against a typewriter; he just went off on it. Yet he never once spoke like that on the bridge. I took a lesson from that. And the one captain who was emotional on the bridge, lashing out in anger or betraying fear in his voice, was the most ineffective man I've ever served with. The entire bridge crew was nervous around him, and it adversely affected our performance.

"So, I resolved that I would always keep my voice steady and calm. I also resolved that I would never let myself grow too close to anyone on the crew—anyone in the service, for that matter—so that they could never see how shaken I get when going into battle or when I have to discipline someone. Mine is more the nature of an engineer than an inspirational figure, and I've often felt deficient in that regard. But given my temperament, it just seems like the best way to manage men in battle." He paused. "I'm afraid that my reserved nature carries over into my personal life as well, and that causes its own set of problems."

Before Easton could say anything, Kendrick concluded with, "Let me say this, John. I've watched how you manage the crew, and you will have no problem in command. It is true that you are more gregarious than I am and that you wear your emotions a little more on your sleeve. But I promise you that when the weight of command falls on your shoulders, you will strike the right balance. The job itself helps you to do that. The thing that matters most is that you care, and that's all a crew really wants from their captain—someone who is aware of their needs and who balances their lives against the demands of the war."

"Thank you, sir. Again, I hope that I didn't offend you."

"Not at all, John. I am who I decided to be, and it has its plusses and minuses. And it's perfectly fine for you to ask me questions about leadership; it is one of my primary responsibilities to prepare men like you for command, so I'm glad you asked me." He reflected for a moment on the advice Easton needed most. "Command is isolating—it has to be. But it has its rewards as well. The truth is that you may be better suited for it than I. I wish I could show emotion more easily." Kendrick smiled. "I guess my biggest regret is that I don't have a typewriter to yell at."

He was pleased when Easton laughed.

"Thank you, sir. I do covet command, but it also makes me nervous."

"Which is why you will be effective at it. John, I do consider you my friend. You are the only one I feel I can talk to with full candor, so thank you for that." Then, realizing that they needed to bring this conversation to an end, Kendrick added, "Which reminds me about that recall of all hands to the ship."

"On it, sir. We'll be ready for whatever happens."

* * *

June 4, 1944—The English Channel

"Now hear this. Now hear this! This is the captain speaking."

Men all over the *Warburton* paused what they were doing to listen to the captain. A crew was always interested in learning their orders, which were seldom shared until the ship was well out to sea and out of range to an idle comment that could be overheard by a spy on land.

"Our task tonight is to drive any U-boats and E-boats from the channel. I know the seas are rough, but we need your utmost diligence in looking for telltale signs of any German craft or activity. If you see something, report it to your officer. This is urgent. That's all!"

"As if any German was going to surface on a night like this!" said one of the mechanic's mates to the chief engineer. "The way we're being tossed around would be fatal for an E-boat, and what U-boat would want to breach the surface when they can hover down below in calm and quiet?"

"Why don't we let the Germans decide what they want to do?" Chief Engineer Calder replied evenly.

"Aye, sir. Just saying."

Calder's shake of the head was enough to bring that conversation to a close.

Up on the bridge, the OOD ordered the helmsman to smarten up on course, which was difficult with the heavy waves coming at them from an angle. It was also unnecessary since the helm was fully aware of the course to follow. But with that much nervous energy on board, people felt the need to say something.

Sensing the tension, Kendrick decided it would be better for all around if he was not on the bridge. Even though they were making a show of force, he also knew that it was highly unlikely the Germans would come out to engage in this weather. Like nearly everyone else in France and Belgium, the German Kriegsmarine had concluded that the window of opportunity for a cross-channel invasion had passed for the month of June, so why risk their lives in bad weather and against the now-undisputed superiority of British and American naval forces?

What was more, the Royal Air Force and US Army Air Corps had complete control of the air over the English Channel. After very nearly crippling the Allied effort with their U-boat campaigns in the first four years of the war, the tide had turned against Germany in the latter half of 1944, and now the number of U-boats deployed was steadily dropping. The war on the eastern front with Russia simply demanded too many resources to allow Germany to fully support the Battle of the Atlantic.

To the OOD, Kendrick said, "I'll be in my cabin. Call at the least sign of trouble."

"Aye, sir. Captain leaving the bridge!"

As Kendrick stepped out into the rain, he felt sick to his stomach—not from the rolling of the ship, although four weeks in port had not been helpful to many of the men who were struggling with seasickness. *I really thought tomorrow was the day.* He shook his head. *We've got to go soon or all those men and support crews on alert will lose momentum.* But as a particularly fierce wave splashed over the side of the ship, drenching him as he raced toward the hatch, he realized that it was futile. Men who were forced to sit in their landing craft on board the larger transport ships would be sicker than dogs in these seas. There was even a risk that many of the flat-bottomed transports would overturn in the waves. "So, not tonight. Probably not this month."

He shook his head again as he closed the door to his cabin behind him. Stripping off his wet clothes, he reached for a towel. "No need for a shower tonight!" The ship lurched with such ferocity that an inexperienced sailor would have been thrown to the floor. But Kendrick simply leaned into it and settled onto his bed. He needed to put on dry clothes so he could be ready to return to the bridge in an instant, even though he knew full well that such a thing was not going to happen. Unbeknownst to the mechanic's mate down below, the captain agreed with the mate's assessment of the Germans' plans for the night. This was a necessary but ultimately unimportant cruise to keep up the appearance that it was business as usual in England, with an invasion force still in the distant future.

* * *

Operation Neptune—June 6, 1944

After a rough but fruitless night at sea on June 4, the men of the *Warburton* were doing their best to get some sleep, with only a minimal crew active during the late-afternoon watch. Among those sleeping was First Officer Easton—until his captain stepped in his room and put an arm on his shoulder. Easton jerked as he was wrenched out of a lurid dream that he really did not want to leave.

"What? What is it?" he asked in that dazed state that accompanies late-in-the-sleep-cycle dreams.

"Sorry, John, but we need to meet with the officers. We have a lot to get ready for."

Easton swung his long legs out from the bed. His six-foot, two-inch frame was nearly a foot longer than the bed in his small cabin, so he spent the night folded into various positions as he tossed and turned. Slender, but well-muscled, he was the type of fellow who looked well put together, even when disheveled by sleep.

"I'll be right there," Easton mumbled.

"Go ahead and take time to wash up. I'd like to meet in fifteen minutes."

"But I'll need to summon the others."

"No, I'm on it. I'll see you in the officers' wardroom." The officers' dining room doubled as a boardroom. Kendrick would make sure the doors were closed so that nosy mess crew members could not listen in. "Even so, they'll figure it out anyway— somehow they always do," he said to himself as he moved down the small corridor to awaken the next man on his list.

Fifteen minutes later, the small group assembled—many at the table, some standing against the walls. The chattering stopped when Kendrick stepped into the room, which was now so packed that it felt like the inside of a crowded elevator without any room to adjust even an elbow. Kendrick motioned for those on the other side of the space to secure the doors. The atmosphere was electric—everyone knew that the invasion was coming sometime—was this finally the time?

"The code name for the action we'll participate in today is *Operation Neptune*, and I just received word that it is officially a go from General Eisenhower, despite the bad weather. Tonight, we will depart for the Normandy beaches at the vanguard of nearly 7,000 ships!" That brought an appreciative murmur— nothing like that had happened in the entire history of the world. Kendrick motioned to restore order. "4,000 of those ships will be troop carriers! Our job is to sweep the ocean ahead of that armada to clear the path of U-boats and drive back any E-boats that might come out to harass the troop carriers." He paused to give his officers a chance to absorb the news.

At first, there was little reaction, perhaps because of his earlier attempt to keep things calm. But then there was a simultaneous intake of breaths, followed by the rise toward a cheer. This time, Kendrick let the group have their cheer. After all they had been through with the Nazis, tonight was the night that the Allies were going to shove it back down their throats, and that was just too much to take in without a cheer.

"Here's the thing," he said after regaining their attention. "7,000 is a lot of ships. Not all will be at sea at the same time, but after the first wave, there will be some ships withdrawing from the beaches while others are approaching. Battleships will stand out to sea to pound the coastal defenses in advance of the landing, and there will be American PT boats and British motor torpedo boats dodging in and out like dogs in a flock of sheep. It is going to be organized chaos. And our job is to weave our way in and out of all of them in our assigned sector, on constant alert for any German counter measures. We are one of sixty-five destroyers, so we must stay inside our lane to not cause confusion. I want you to double our usual lookouts and make sure communications between everyone involved in navigation and steering is as close to instantaneous and flaw-free as possible."

People nodded.

"And be adaptable. There has never been a naval operation as large as this one, and while destroyers are not the center of the show, we have a role to play. Let's do it right. We'll depart at 2200 and stay in action throughout most of the night and following day, so figure out how to keep the men up and at it." He paused. "One last thing—nothing like this has ever been done before. We're about to make history, so each of you do your part!"

This was met with another cheer. When at last they quieted, he dismissed them to go to their various command centers to map out strategies and determine when to brief their crew. This time, there would be no general announcements, even when at sea.

* * *

"Message from Admiral Bryant, sir!"

Kendrick grabbed the paper from the signalman and began reading intensely. The morning had not gone well. The *Warburton* had departed Portland at 2200 the night of June 5, making its way toward the westernmost landing beaches, which had been designated Omaha and Utah by those responsible for generating code names. The British were landing at three beaches to the east—Gold, Juno, and Sword—and it was up to the Americans to make their way across the broad beaches of Utah and up the vertical cliffs of Pointe du Hoc at Omaha. The problems started almost immediately.

While the weather *did* moderate from the fierce storms of June 4 and 5, the seas were still rough, with long, rolling swells in the darkness on June 6. That made life miserable for the more than 150,000 soldiers who were put out to sea shortly after midnight. By the time the landing crafts arrived at the beaches at 0630 in the morning, most of the men were overwhelmed by seasickness. The next problem to surface was that the severe weather had caused many of the troop carriers to drift off station. Men were being landed far from their originally assigned spot. Military units were split up such that leadership was scrambled. And worst of all, from the point of view of the men on the *Warburton*, it seemed the heavy pre-invasion aircraft bombardment and the pre-dawn heavy bombardment by the battleships had failed to knock out the German gun emplacements situated above the beaches and cliffs. They knew this because as they drew close to shore, they could see American soldiers being cut down almost the moment they landed. It was a horrifying sight to see German gunners protected inside heavy concrete gun emplacements firing down on the defenseless invaders.

"Attention on deck!" Kendrick shouted. He was not usually one to shout, so this got everyone's attention very quickly. "I want to read you the orders I just received from Rear Admiral Carleton Bryant. 'Get on them, men! Get on them! They are raising hell with the men on the beach, and we can't have any more of that! We must stop it!'" Kendrick choked up. "That's it, men. We have to go into shore and start firing on the German fixed positions. Helm, bring us to course 180—due south to France! All-ahead half-speed."

"Aye, sir. Come to course 180 and all-ahead half-speed."

"Very good."

"Sonar, give me continual depth soundings. I want to go in as close as possible without touching bottom. It's your job to keep us safe."

"Aye, sir. Continuous soundings!"

The adrenaline surging in the room was contagious as everyone leaned forward to watch the beach come closer and closer.

Kendrick turned to Easton. "I wish we could go in at flank speed, but it's going to get shallow pretty quick, and the Germans have placed a lot of their underwater steel tripods and Czech hedgehogs to poke holes in our landing craft. I don't want to get fouled in any of their contraptions."

"Yes, sir." Easton was as anxious as Kendrick. Their view of the threats the American GIs were facing became clearer with each moment as they drew closer to the beach.

"I'm stepping outside. Care to join me?" Kendrick asked.

"Yes, sir." The two men moved onto the wing next to the enclosed bridge. They heard a ping, which prompted Kendrick to step to the side.

"All stop!" Kendrick shouted.

"All stop!"

"Very well."

"Was that a rifle shell?" Easton asked.

"I think so!" Kendrick said, laughing. "I guess we're close enough. Obviously, some of the Germans onshore don't like us being here." He moved back into the protection of the bridge, but Easton stayed outside. "Mr. Pendleton."

"Sir!"

"Use your judgment to find targets for our five-inch guns to fire on," Kendrick commanded. "Try to spot the places where you see smoke or flashes from the German occupied ground, and then fire away at those spots. Let's give our men on the beach some covering fire."

"Aye, sir." Pendleton moved quickly to his control station, where he started reaching out to the gun crews. Within a matter of moments, he was directing fire against German shore emplacements. The sound of their own guns going off was very heartening to the entire crew, and a cheer went up when a puff of smoke indicated that one of their shells blew up a machine-gun nest at the base of one of the inlets to the beach.

"Good shooting, Mr. Pendleton!"

Pendleton turned and gave a thumbs-up.

Kendrick stepped onto the deck again, where Easton still stood. At this point, there was no threat of attack on the *Warburton* by the German Kriegsmarine. No submarine could come this close, and if any had been present that morning, they would have already attacked the battleships for maximum damage. But the Battle of the Atlantic had been so effective that not a single German submarine was detected anywhere among the armada. Earlier, Kendrick had received reports that four German E-boats had ventured out that morning, successfully attacking a Norwegian warship with torpedoes, but it was also reported they had turned tail and ran as soon as a destroyer started after them. The Allied fleet's only risk now was from an aerial bombardment, given that they had no maneuverability at all while this close to shore. But so far, the Luftwaffe was also missing in action.

"What are you looking at, John?"

"It's strange, sir," Easton said. "Do you see the *USS Carmick* over there?"

"Yes—she's commanded by Robert Beer, an excellent leader."

"I've been watching how they place their fire. It looks to me like they use spotters to see where some of the American tanks on shore are firing, and then the *Carmick* fires on the same position with their larger guns."

"Really?" Kendrick raised his binoculars to watch the action. Sure enough, he saw a Sherman tank on the beach fire up into a draw, and then he watched as the *Carmick* let loose on the same spot with their weapons. "Fascinating!" he said.

"What?"

"I believe that this is intentional—it's not simply the spotters providing additional artillery support, I think the *Carmick* is using the *tanks* as spotters for where to direct their fire."

"You think?" Easton watched another round of fire. "Well, I'll be. You must be right. Since we have no radio communication with the shore units, they've figured out an informal way to communicate with those on shore to coordinate the attack."

"Oh, this is exciting," Kendrick said. He moved quickly to the fire-control station and motioned for Pendleton. "Don, you've got to see this!" When he pointed out the pattern the *Carmick* followed, Pendleton whistled.

"Well, I'll be! If that isn't the smartest thing I've ever seen."

"Can we match it? There's no way to let the people on shore know what we're doing, other than to match their fire."

"We have two tanks firing in our sector. They're both under heavy fire. I'll get right on it." With that, he contacted his assigned spotters and instructed them to watch where the tanks were firing. Once that information was relayed down, he gave the coordinates to the two forward five-inch MK-12 main batteries.

Within a matter of moments, Pendleton's guns fired on the exact same spot. At least one of their rounds was successful as a small geyser of concrete and machine-gun parts erupted into the air. Pendleton, Kendrick, and Easton all watched to see what would happen next.

The tanks, which had been firing at regular intervals, hesitated. Then the two tanks separated. One of them backed up a bit, raised its gun barrel to maximum elevation, and fired into the side of the cliff. Kendrick wanted more than anything to tell Pendleton that they were trying to signal to fire at the top of the cliff, but it was not his call to make. Even so, he shouldn't have worried. In a few moments, he heard the forward-most gun fire at the spot, and then a cloud erupted at the top of the hill. Another seven or eight rounds, and suddenly, all enemy fire from that position came to an end.

In the meantime, the other tank had moved closer into shore and could be seen lumbering its way into the small creek that led from the land onto the beach and into the ocean. The easiest way for ground troops to advance off the beach was up the V created by the erosion from this stream, but the Germans had placed concrete barriers to trap tanks and troops in this spot. German machine-gun emplacements on either side could then fire down on the American troops, and Germans armed with bazookas could fire on the tanks. The lone G.I. tank swiveled its barrel in such a way as to reveal the German positions.

"Okay, this one is really tricky," Kendrick said to Easton. "We know where they want us to fire, but if any of our assault troops have crawled their way up from the beach, they will be in the line of our fire."

Should they fire in such a broad pattern?

Luckily, the answer came quickly. This time, the chief gunnery officer directed the three batteries aft to lay down a broadside against all the positions indicated by the tank. In quick succession, a series of explosions on the beach threw up sand, debris, and mangled equipment. The tank swiveled its barrel to the same positions again and fired, which they interpreted as a request to repeat the exercise.

At this point, Kendrick could not stand it any longer, so he moved into the fire-control station next to Pendleton. "It looks like they liked what you did on that last salvo."

"Yes, sir. I'm going to fire on the same positions but just a bit farther from the beach. We'll also fire just a few feet forward. I'm going to use three times as many shells. That way we should create a pattern that will hit the Germans wherever they happen to be." He looked at Kendrick, as if for permission.

"Carry on, Don! This is your show."

Pendleton nodded and gave the orders. The five-inch guns began a series of rapid-fire patterns that quickly obliterated that part of the beach. On shore, the tank acknowledged this new round by moving closer to the draw to see if it drew any fire. When a flash was seen on the cliff well above the draw and to the left, Pendleton immediately ordered his forward batteries to fire on that spot. Soon, the top of the cliff was engulfed in flame, and the firing stopped.

"I know it moves so fast, sir, that it's hard to keep track. But we have now fired more than 800 rounds. We were told to keep at least half our remaining rounds available in case of an emergency. If we follow that directive, I should stop this support right now, and you should probably move farther out to sea."

Kendrick motioned for Easton to join them. He had Pendleton repeat his ammunition status to update Easton.

"I don't know about you two," Kendrick said quietly, "but watching what those men on the beach have been going through seems like an emergency to me. What do you think?"

"I say we stay and fight," Easton said. "We now have a means of identifying targets, and our guns are far more accurate than the indiscriminate fire from the battleships earlier this morning. It's too late in the battle for bomber aircraft to provide the kind of precision support they need. Let's give it to them. Those are American boys out there!"

"Thank you. Don, what do you think?"

"I think it's a once-in-a-lifetime opportunity to direct our fire where we know it's doing some good. With your permission, I'd like to continue the fight."

"I agree completely. Mr. Pendleton, continue to fire until we are down to 200 rounds or the tanks are able to move up and off the beach—whichever comes first."

Pendleton smiled. A rare opportunity indeed. "Aye, sir! Now if you'll excuse me . . ." And he turned away to get back to his job.

"Let's go outside and watch again," Kendrick suggested.

Easton and Kendrick moved to the open deck.

"I have an idea, sir."

"I'm interested."

"If German rifle fire can reach us, why can't our 20-millimeters lay down some covering fire as well? Once we have cleared the beach with our five-inch guns, we can maneuver to port where it looks like they are having a rough go of it because of low-lying German machine-gun emplacements."

"Worth a try. Please go discuss this with Pendleton. If he agrees, you give the order."

"Aye, sir."

That was the second officer Kendrick had made smile in as many minutes. In what was probably one of the most historic days in the long history of warfare, the crews of the American destroyers were playing a new and unexpected role—one that was to prove decisive in completing the Operation Neptune portion of the larger Operation Overlord invasion of mainland Europe.

Twenty minutes later, the *Warburton* made the change so that their 20-millimeter guns could lay down fire. The impact on the beach was immediate as American GIs started moving forward under this new blizzard of support.

Kendrick turned to Easton to compliment him. But as he turned, a spray of blood splattered his face. A German sniper had sighted in on them; Easton had just been hit in the skull with a high-velocity shell. He fell backward without a sound as Kendrick ducked behind the protective cowling.

Kendrick heard himself screaming as he started dragging Easton's body back toward the protection of the bridge. He couldn't tell if the moisture on his face was from his own tears or John Easton's blood. Of course, it did not matter. His friend was dead, and his ship was in danger.

"Corpsman! I need a corpsman!" Kendrick shouted. But it would do no good. He knew that but was simply not ready to let go. "Oh, John, I am so sorry." Kendrick felt his throat tighten as a wave of despair washed over him, unlike anything he'd experienced before. "Oh, John."

CHAPTER THIRTEEN
AN EARLY END

"Sorry about your first officer."

"Yes, sir. Thank you." Kendrick paused so that he could say the next words without choking up, but it did not fully work. "He was an excellent officer and a good friend." Kendrick did not add that he found it hard to make friends, so John's death was even more of a challenge for him.

Admiral Luekenga nodded. "But what a remarkably successful mission you had. It turns out our little destroyer group was a key element in the success of the landings."

Several days had passed since the mission, and more than 300,000 Allied troops had been landed. Kendrick knew the number would eventually exceed over 1.5 million before Operation Overload, the overarching mission of which Neptune was a part, concluded. The Allies were on the mainland, and the Germans would never again dislodge them.

"I understand that our forces in the Mediterranean are on alert," Kendrick said.

"I don't know too much about that yet. But Churchill never wanted the Normandy invasion—he thought the cost in men's lives would be too great. So my guess is that there is something brewing in the south. I can say that we've been sending a great deal of equipment and material that way." Luekenga was wise enough to know that Kendrick was positioning for a transfer to that theater—after all, it was likely to have the next big impact on the war from a naval point of view.

"And the Pacific continues to heat up."

Luekenga couldn't help but laugh. All destroyer captains were the same, always angling for the best posting. "Yes, the Pacific war is truly a naval war. No continent to invade—just some small islands with a lot of fanatical defenders. We have our hands full there."

Kendrick nodded, wondering where the *Warburton* would go next.

"But unfortunately, you won't be going to either theater."

"What?" Kendrick coughed. "I mean, what, sir?"

Luekenga motioned for Kendrick to sit down. "I received a telegram from the War Department this morning. It should have gone to you first, but they could get it to me faster because of our secure lines. Your grandfather has had a heart attack, and the War Department wants you to return to New York as soon as possible."

"My grandfather!" Kendrick's mind reeled. "Does it say how he's doing?"

Rather than respond, Luekenga simply handed the piece of paper to Kendrick:

> Please notify Commander Merrill Kendrick that Edgar Kendrick has suffered heart attack. STOP. Condition stable. STOP. Request you approve immediate transfer to New York for assistance at Gatekeeper Electrics. STOP.

Kendrick took a deep breath. "So, my service as a destroyer captain is over."

"At least for now. You have an important company to run. I should have sent you home earlier."

"I should have requested a transfer earlier. Staying here was unfair to my grandfather." He looked down at his hands, then up at Luekenga. "But this is important too."

"I've got you a seat on an army air corps cargo plane that is flying to New York this afternoon, leaving Portsmouth and refueling in Helsinki. You should be home by tomorrow."

Merrill Kendrick stood. "Thank you, sir. I appreciate that." He hesitated for a moment. "I never wanted to run a company."

"I'd think of it as just another command assignment if I were in your shoes. A company is like a ship: people who need supervision, facilities that empower your mission but must be maintained, and goals and objectives to be fulfilled. There are many ways to fight a war, Merrill, and who's to say which element is most important?"

"Yes, sir. Thank you. It's been an honor to serve with you."

Luekenga came around the desk and extended his hand. "With you as well. You are a courageous and bold leader. You made a real difference in the prosecution of the war. We'll miss you."

Kendrick and Luekenga saluted each other, then Kendrick turned and left the room. As he walked along the wharf to collect his things, his mind wandered.

"I would have recommended you for command of the *Warburton*, John. She was yours by right." He bit his lower lip. "But now she belongs to someone else." As he approached the ship, he hesitated for a moment so he could burn the scene into his memory. "My father thinks you are below our station, but to me, you are the finest warship of all. Right into the mouth of the enemy." He stopped talking. The ship knew all of this because it was the embodiment of all who served in this fight for freedom. He thought of all the men he had served with. He thought of all who were killed or injured. And then he saluted the *Warburton*. His ship no more. "Destroyers and U-boats—

we both had a role to play." He inhaled to steady his voice. "I'm glad we destroyers were victorious!"

Then Merrill Kendrick, now president and chief executive officer of Gatekeeper Electrics, moved forward to assume his new role in life.

AUTHOR'S NOTES

DARK SEAS IS MY TWENTIETH published book; I've written ten nonfiction biographies and ten historical novels. Thirteen were written as tributes to the men and women who have served America in wartime, including this book. I am continually grateful for the courage and sacrifice of those who serve in uniform to protect our freedom and way of life.

The characters in *Dark Seas* are fictional, as are the battle scenes and the fraud attributed to Gatekeeper Electrics. But the scenes are accurate in describing the actual types of battles that occurred between destroyers and U-boats and surface craft in the Battle of the Atlantic. I did my very best to help you feel what it was like to be on the bridge of a destroyer in battle, including the uncertainty, anxiety, and exhaustion of staying at battle stations for hours on end. It was grueling—and heroic!

Unfortunately, war profiteering has occurred in all wars in recorded history. There is a great deal of money involved in making war, and there have always been unscrupulous people who defraud the military—often putting lives at risk through their defective supplies and service. The story of Gatekeeper Electrics was intended to convey this cost while honoring those who resisted the temptation to cheat. I thought it might be an unfamiliar part of the war story to many readers.

The chapter relative to destroyer support for the Normandy landings at Omaha and Utah Beaches is inspired by actual events. The *USS Carmick* and its captain, Robert Beer, were real, and they were the first to figure out the firing pattern directed by tanks on the beach. Their contribution to saving American lives was immeasurable. Also, the order from Rear Admiral Carleton Bryant is authentic: "Get on them men! Get on them! They are raising hell with the men on the beach, and we can't have any more of that! We must stop it!" The destroyers' response to this order was astonishingly successful and heroic in its execution.

In my previous military novels, I've included scenes from battleships, aircraft carriers, motor torpedo boats, and submarines. I thought it was time that I research and pay tribute to the "tin can" warriors who served on the relatively small destroyers who punched far above their weight class in terms of their contribution to the successful prosecution of the war at sea.

ABOUT THE AUTHOR

JERRY BORROWMAN IS AN AWARD-WINNING author of World War II coauthored biographies, including *Three Against Hitler* with Rudi Wobbe and *A Distant Prayer* with Joseph Banks. He's also a best-selling fiction writer, having written the popular four-book series starting with the World War I novel *'Til the Boys Come Home*, and the Depression-era novel *One Last Chance*. *Stories from the Life of Porter Rockwell* was his first writing outside the twentieth century and opened a whole new world to his writing and to his own pioneer family. Jerry and Marcella are the parents of four children and five grandchildren.

Compassionate Soldier earned Jerry the prestigious George Washington Medal of Honor from the Freedoms Foundation at Valley Forge because of the quality of his narrative in sharing the real-life stories of heroic men and women who sacrificed their safety to help others, even in the midst of war. It also took first place (Gold) in the Foreword Reviews 2018 Indie Awards in the category of Military and War.

Visit www.jerryborrowman.com to learn more.